Jack Adrift

My Life as it Is

Ms. Noelle is sick and tired of me. She never looks me in the eye anymore. She never calls on me. I even think she grades me more harshly. The other day I had a nose bleed. Blood was pouring out of me like a busted hose and all she could say was, "Go stand on your head for a while."

I brought her flowers I took from the cemetary next door. She didn't even bother to put them into water. By the end of the day they were as dead as where they came from. As dead as she wanted me, I think.

Part of my trouble started when I snuck up on her at the grocery store. "Hi, Ms. Noelle," I shouted.

Jack Adrift
Fourth Grade without a Clue

...new suede shoes. Then I saw her at the drug store. She was talking to the pharmacist when I creeped up behind her and said, "Peek-a-boo!" She nearly jumped a foot and quickly shoved something down into her purse.

"Jack!" she said briskly, "please don't sneak up on me..."

Farrar, Straus and Giroux   New York

Copyright © 2003 by Jack Gantos
All rights reserved
Distributed in Canada by Douglas & McIntyre Ltd.
Printed in the United States of America
Designed by Nancy Goldenberg
First edition, 2003
5 7 9 10 8 6

Library of Congress Cataloging-in-Publication Data
Gantos, Jack.
  Jack Adrift : fourth grade without a clue / Jack Gantos.— 1st ed.
    p. cm.
  Summary: When his father rejoins the Navy and moves the family to
Cape Hatteras, North Carolina, nine-year-old Jack becomes confused by
a crush on his teacher, contradictory advice from his parents, and a very
strange neighbor.
  ISBN 0-374-39987-5
  [1. Teacher-student relationships—Fiction.   2. Family life—North
Carolina—Fiction.   3. Schools—Fiction.   4. Moving, Household—
Fiction.   5. North Carolina—Fiction.] I. Title.

PZ7.G15334Jaak 2003
[Fic]—dc21

                                                           2002192880

For Anne and Mabel

Contents

It was family open house day at the Sea Bees base. Dad made Pete and me wear our Jr. Naval Cadets outfits. Julian was coming with us because his Dad was setting up the band for a Sea Beats concert and his Mom was decorating the stage with giant musical notes wearing Navy caps. Julian was off the charts crazy because his Dad promised he would play one of Julian's songs.

"Which one?" I asked.

"It's top secret," he replied.

On the way to the base Mom and Betsy held their hands out the windows to let their wet nail polish dry. As soon as we parked Julian jumped out of the car and ran toward the bandstand. People had already filled the rows of folding chairs. In a minute Jillian came running back.

"Disaster!" he shouted. "The band blew a fuse while warming up and it will take a while to fix."

The next thing I knew Dad was on the stage. He cupped his hands aroun_____ ___th. "Welcome to SeaBee_____ _____ hollered. "While_____ _____ 'and to begin _____ _____ arm you all up with a ____le story."

The crowd groaned a bit but that didn't slow Dad down. "Once, a long time ago," he began, "a father and son traveled a long way to buy a donkey. Once they bought him they began to walk him home. Along the way they passed through a town and the people laughed at them. "Don't you know you are sopped to ride the donkey," they said. So the father got on the donkey. In the next town the people were upset with the father. "Let the boy ride," they shouted. The father traded places with his son. In the third town the people yelled, "Idiot, the two of you can ride the donkey." So the father and son rode together. In the fourth town the people were outraged. "Look at that poor donkey," they said. "You should carry him." So the father and son carried the donkey, and he was very heavy. Finally, they were crossing the last bridge when they dropped the donkey in the water. "See," said the father, "When you listen to others you can lose your

The whole family was in the big white Buick Roadmaster convertible, which was as round and long as a whale out of water. My older sister, Betsy, named it Moby Dick and after twenty hours on the road Dad looked as bug-eyed behind the wheel as Captain Ahab. Dad had just bought it with bonus money the Navy gave him for enlisting in the Seabees, which was the branch of the Navy that built anything ships and sailors needed at their home base or when they docked at a port. Back in our small hometown he was a house builder and he thought this Navy stint would give us all a fresh start because, as he explained it to us one night over dinner, "We don't stand a snowball's chance of ever getting ahead while living out here in the sticks where people dig coal, eat squirrels, and build more *outhouses* than people houses."

He was right. If we stayed out in the sticks we'd just be stuck there forever. But Mom had always lived out in

the sticks and she didn't want to leave her family behind. Still, Dad had a point. He looked Mom in the eye
and waved his fork at us kids. "Do you want Betsy to
have to clean other people's houses for a living? Or Pete
to be a fruit picker? Or have Jack junior here grow up
like your brother Jim, who has to shoot coal-mine rats
for a living?"

I wouldn't have minded shooting rats for a living, but
Mom agreed with Dad that our futures would be
brighter elsewhere, so they decided we should become a
Navy family and make the move to Cape Hatteras. We
sold all our furniture and just brought Dad's tools, the
kitchen and bathroom stuff, and our clothes. It all fit
easily into the Roadmaster's trunk, which was as roomy
as a walk-in closet.

On the AAA map, North Carolina didn't seem far
away from our town south of Pittsburgh. But on the
road, we ran into a lot of construction and it was slow
going. Still, the car was comfortable, and with the top
up it smelled just like when you open a book for the
first time, which kept the trip fresh and full of hope. In
the backseat we played cards and travel games and did
a lot of singing and then gradually we all started to fade.
We got tired and pasty and worn-out and we flopped
around and squabbled over pillows and kicked at each
other for more space. The Roadmaster no longer felt
roomy as we fell into a long period of grumpy silence.

Then, after a catnap, I thought I'd start a little conversation and perk everyone up again. But my conversational effort turned into a disaster. All I said was, "I'm a little concerned about how to make friends in a new place. Does anyone have any advice?" Well, that opened the floodgates to a nose-to-nose disagreement between Mom and Dad.

At first, all Dad said was, "The secret to making new friends is exactly the same secret as how to be a success in life—you just look people right in the eye and tell them what they want to hear. You'll make all the friends you want and cut through life like a hot knife through butter."

"I disagree entirely," Mom said, alarmed. She turned toward me. "The best way to make friends and sail through life is to always be yourself. And that is not a *secret*. Everybody knows honesty is the best policy."

"You mean a policy for people who don't have any ambition," Dad said. Lately he worked the word *ambition* into every conversation.

"No," she said, raising her voice, "ambition is no excuse to turn your back on honesty and self-respect."

Betsy groaned. *"See what you started,"* she hissed, then slumped down in her seat and looked miserable.

"Self-respect is overrated," Dad shot back. "I always feel a lot better when I get exactly what I want. Only whiners sit around worrying about *self-respect*."

"Well, that is one of the fundamental differences between us," Mom declared. "You have no respect for the truth. You'll say *anything* to get what you want and I won't stoop to such low-life tricks." Then she turned back to me. "My dad never told a lie in his life," she said with great pride.

"And where'd that get him?" Dad asked.

"He's a pillar of the community," Mom said proudly. "And people want to be his friend because they know he won't lie to them, and feed them a load of you know what . . ."

"The only load of you know what is what you are telling Jack—"

Mom cut him off. "I don't want to talk about this nonsense anymore," she said, dicing the air with her words.

Suddenly, instead of feeling like I was riding a whale, I felt swallowed by it. But I did start thinking about what they had said. I had seen both of them tell stories, and they each had a different style. Dad would say anything to keep people on the edge of their seats. Every time he went to the Elks Club he'd draw a crowd, tell wild stories, and drink for free. Once in a while he'd take me, so I got to see him in action. When we'd enter the club he'd give me a dollar in quarters and send me to a far corner to play the pinball machines. He'd lean on the bar and tell a story to the bartender. Then the bartender would start to gather a crowd. "Get over here," he'd holler to a few guys who were bored and staring down into their beers. "You gotta hear this story. Go ahead, Jack," he'd say as the men moved closer to Dad, "tell it again." And with each good laugh a few more guys pulled up chairs and drinks and Dad jumped into action again, telling more outrageous stories and giving the crowd just what they wanted—a thrill. They didn't seem to care if the stories were true or not.

On the other hand I had been with Mom when she was telling a story about her *Mayflower* relatives to the well-dressed ladies down at the Daughters of the American Revolution headquarters. It was all I could do to keep from falling asleep as she went on and on about every little family-tree detail, and then she would pause for a minute and roll her eyes up into her head to sort out some fact in her mind until she got it all straight and then would inch forward again. And even though the D.A.R. ladies were polite, I could spot their necks flexing and faces swelling out from stifled yawns . . .

After a while the road began to dip down, then rise up, and then dip down as if we were driving across the ocean. Suddenly my little brother, Pete, bleated, "I don't feel too good." I heard something surging up his throat and quickly grabbed him by the hair and yanked his face toward his sneakers. He missed me but sprayed his shoes, and with a follow-up blast he made a chocolate

brown puddle, colorfully speckled with some undi-
gested M&M's, on the floor behind Dad's seat. Even
though it was kind of pretty puke, it smelled toxic.

Dad smoothly pulled over to the side of the road. He
hopped out of the car and opened the trunk. Mom
leaned way over her seat and patted Pete on his sweaty
head.

"You'll be fine," she said. "It was just a little motion
sickness, but now it's over with. Happens to the best of
us."

I wondered if Mom was telling Pete what he wanted
to hear, or if she was telling the truth. If he threw up
again would he think she was lying? Because I already
knew that part of what she said was a lie—*I* never had
motion sickness and *I* was better than he was, so it
didn't always happen to "the best of us."

Dad opened Pete's door and caught a fresh whiff of
the puke. "Holy mackerel!" he cried out, and took a
deep breath before leaning in and sopping it up with a
car rag. When he finished cleaning up, he tossed the
rag in a ditch by the side of the road and wiped his
hands on the grass.

"Time to lower the roof and air this big boy out," he
said to no one in particular. He unhooked the chrome
clamps above the sun visors and lifted the stiff top. It
folded back like an accordion and Dad stuffed it down

into a gap behind the backseat and snapped it into place under a white vinyl cover. It was so cool.

When he got back into his seat, he put the car in gear and we merged with the ongoing traffic. The road construction was behind us and he hit the gas. It felt like we were in a wind tunnel. Mom had one hand holding down her plaid floppy summer hat while the fingers of her other hand dug into Dad's shoulder. Betsy sat squinting unhappily, fighting a desperate battle to keep her long black hair from constantly whipping across her eyes. A hurricane had swept the coast two days before and the trailing clouds were still bloated and low, and it was threatening to rain. Lightning slashed above the distant trees. Wet leaves flattened against the windshield. Still, it was thrilling to see everything so clearly with the top down. Then, just when I thought no one would ever speak again, Dad cleared the air with an upbeat remark.

"This baby has a *nose* for the ocean," he said proudly, steering toward Cape Hatteras with one hand on the wheel and the other loosely hanging down over the outside of the door like shark bait. He was eager to get over the Wright Brothers Memorial Bridge and to the Outer Banks before nightfall.

When we reached the bridge there was a Coast Guard sailor on sentry duty. A black-and-white-striped sawhorse blocked the road and the sailor lazily waved a long flashlight with a glowing orange rim over his head. Dad slowed down and pulled toward him.

"The bridge is closed," the sailor announced, chewing on a huge wad of gum which caused his cheek muscles to throb and flex like a human heart. "The water hasn't pulled back all the way since the storm. Still about six inches over the roads."

Dad pulled out his Navy identification card and showed it to the guard. "Cape Hatteras is my new assignment," he said. "I'm supposed to be on-site tomorrow."

The guard hesitated. "I don't know," he said, with his jaws pumping blood to his brain. "That's a lot of water."

"Mister, I'm in the *Navy*," Dad said. "Six inches isn't enough to drown in. Besides, this Buick is more boat than car. A few inches of water can't scuttle us."

"Then help yourself," the sailor said, turning to lift the sawhorse barrier to one side. As we passed by he called out, "Hope you have some life jackets."

Mom looked spooked. "Honey, do we have life jackets?"

"Just use your seat cushion," Dad suggested, and laughed. He was in a great mood.

We slowly motored up the bridge as if we were clanking our way up the log flume ride at an amusement park.

"See!" Dad shouted into the wind. "What I told the guard back there is a perfect example of what I said earlier. I don't have to be at work for a week, but I had to tell that sailor what he wanted to hear or else he'd've had us spend the night in a motel as if we had money to burn."

"Jack senior," Mom said sharply, getting stirred up again, "that's called lying."

"No," Dad replied, "that's called getting what you want from someone too stupid to give it to you in the first place."

"Don't listen to him," Mom said. Pete wasn't because he was so sick. Betsy wasn't because she was wearing her miserable face again, which meant she wouldn't listen even if you pressed a bullhorn against her ear and shouted, "I'M A JERK! HIT ME!" But I was listening to Dad a lot because I was trying to figure out who I was, and how to be. School was starting in a few days and I expected the local kids were going to be staring at me, then whispering among themselves, then approaching me, then they'd want to know who I was, where I came from, and did I have any hobbies or favorite sports, or was I good at anything at all? I knew it would be a lot easier to take Dad's advice and just make up something incredible they would think was cool. Or, I could simply tell them the truth, the whole truth, and nothing but the truth, which is that I am totally *boring*.

When we reached the top of the bridge, Dad stopped and we looked down on the Outer Banks. We gasped. There was no land. The bridge just slanted down into the water like a boat slip. I knew it wasn't deep, though, because all the houses were above water and I could see where the sea lapped up to their first doorsteps. Still, it looked like we were getting ready to drive right across the Atlantic Ocean toward France.

Mom smacked her lips in the nervous way she does before saying something that might rattle Dad and set him off. "Are you sure it's safe to go down there?"

Dad grinned. "You never know till you try it," he said gleefully, and lifted his foot off the brake. The car tilted forward and began to pick up speed.

"Jack," Dad hollered, "if Pete has to tip his bucket again, just aim his mouth overboard."

"Aye-aye, Captain," I called back, and gave him a snappy salute. I was ready to join the Navy myself.

"Betsy," Dad said, catching her scowling face in the rearview mirror, "get ready to bail."

"Can I just *bail* myself out of here?" she said as she glowered.

The car was humming down the bridge and by the time we hit the bottom our faces were all pulled back in absolute terror. We screamed. The water splashed up in front of us and a shower sprayed back over the windshield, and for a moment the car seemed to glide

weightlessly across the surface before settling down on
the asphalt. The sailor had been right. The water was
only about six inches deep. "We're here," Dad announced, as he slowly navigated along the faint center
line just visible under the water. Behind us our wake
spread out as if we were in a boat.

"Now let's see if we can find our street," he said. "It's
supposed to be somewhere off of Virginia Dare Trail."
After we all caught our breaths, we called out the names
of streets as we trolled along.

"Too bad I don't have a fishing pole," Dad said. "We
could catch dinner on the way to the house."

"You could tie a line to the radio antenna," I suggested.

"Yeah," he added, "we'll have to get some surf-casting
poles and I can show you how to catch a big one."

Or just *say* that you caught a big one, I thought.

Just then we passed a school and a cemetery. I wondered if that was my school and if I would flunk out and
end up next door in the graveyard. The white crosses
and mossy tombstones seemed like the tips of ghostly
topmasts and flags over sunken ships. "Once during a
flood when I was a kid," Dad said joyfully, "coffins
popped right out of the ground and we paddled them
around like canoes."

"*Jack,*" Mom cried out, and elbowed him, "that can't
be true!"

"Sure it is," he said with a laugh. "Would I lie to you?"

I wanted to find a coffin. Maybe Dad would let me tie it to the back of the car and I could ride it. But I didn't spot anything floating around the cemetery except for plastic flowers, garbage, and clumps of seaweed.

There were no other cars on the road.

A few people had stayed and their lights were on. Some were sweeping water out their front doors. When they looked up at us, we waved and they waved back. Wet carpets were stretched across sagging clotheslines. Sand bags edged the yard of a big house, but the water still got through. A banner in front of a cottage the size of a kid's playhouse read: WE SURVIVED! BUT THE STORM BLEW AWAY!

"These people are nuts," Dad declared. "I wouldn't stay out here in a storm."

"What are people going to say when they wake up or return and find us here?" Mom said. "They'll think we are a bunch of sea monkeys."

"Yeah," Betsy said, perking up, "they'll throw a net over us and call the aquarium."

"Or the funny farm," Mom added.

"Early to bed, early to rise makes a man healthy, wealthy, and wise," Dad said confidently, as if quoting one of the Ten Commandments.

"That's right," I chimed. "The early bird gets the worm."

Betsy squinted angrily at me. "Don't *humor him*," she whispered.

A long time passed and we didn't find our street name but finally we spotted a blue-and-white sign that read: SEABEE HOUSING. WELCOME, SAILORS!

"That's us," Dad said merrily, pointing. There were five long house trailers that looked as if they were set down in the middle of a swamp of thick reeds, saw grass, and scrawny, windblown trees. We almost missed the trailers because they were painted in green-and-tan camouflage.

"One of these must be ours," Dad said, looking over a letter with his instructions.

Mom snatched the letter out of his hands. "It can't be," she said, reading it quickly. "It's sitting in a swamp."

"That's not a swamp," Dad replied, waving toward the house trailer. "It's probably a tidal pool. Something educational for the kids."

"Something to immunize them against," Mom said. "I won't live in one of these shoe boxes."

Dad ignored that statement and pulled the letter back out of her hands. "Says here number three is ours."

"I can't believe we've traveled this far to live like trash

in a swamp," Mom said, getting a bit huffy. "If my father saw this he'd . . ."

Betsy glanced over at me. "Here we go again," she sang, as if it were my fault.

"Now don't feel bad," Dad replied. "We're all in the same boat. It's just temporary Navy housing."

"Well *I* didn't join the Navy," she said.

"You did worse," Dad said with a laugh. "You married the Navy, which is ten times as bad 'cause you don't even get paid."

"Yeah," she said without much humor. "And now that I've been captured I'm being tortured, too."

"Yep," Dad said. "You'll just have to show some grit, because the Geneva convention doesn't cover marriage."

Mom reached over and pinched him until he hollered. That must have made her feel a little better because she did show some grit. She always tried to make the best of a bad situation. "There's number three," she said. "Dock this boat and let's go see just how bad it is."

Dad drove up to the front door. If I'd had a rope I would have run a line from the hood ornament to the doorknob to keep us from drifting out to sea.

Dad took off his shoes and socks, hopped out, and sloshed his way around the car. He picked Mom up like a new bride and carried her up the few steps. She reached out and turned the doorknob. It was unlocked and they stepped right in. A moment later the lights inside began to come on. I peeled off my shoes and socks and Pete crawled onto my back. "Puke on my head and I'll drop you," I said, as I carried him through the water.

"Drop me and I'll need mouth-to-mouth resuscitation," he gurgled.

That was a disgusting thought.

Betsy sat in the car by herself, pouting. I knew she was wishing for the worst and had her fingers crossed that things inside the house would be so bad we'd all just run screaming back to the car, and Dad would drive down the road and over the bridge and all the way back to our hometown, where Betsy had a million great friends. I knew how she felt. I was leaving my friends behind, too. But since she was three years older than me she knew hers longer, and because of that I figured she'd miss them more.

But the little house wasn't so bad. The Navy had filled it with new furniture and carpets. As Mom said, "It's not fancy, but its good *family* furniture." There were clean pillows and linens folded on the fresh mattresses, and the bathroom was spotless. The kitchen was small, but everything in it was spick-and-span. There was a new couch with a matching coffee table and lamps.

Pete threw himself on the couch like a dead dog lying on its back, with its legs straight up in the air.

"If you have to be sick, do it in the bathroom," Mom insisted.

"There's no TV," he whined. "I'll never get better."

"You don't need one," Dad said. "TV is only for people who are stuck out in the sticks. *We* are in Cape Hatteras! There are millions of things to do here."

I looked out the front window to see if I could find some of the millions of things to do. Across the street was a Gulf gas station. The sun had almost faded and the round orange Gulf sign shined orangely onto my face. "It looks like a giant orange lollipop," I said to Betsy, who had finally given up and come into the house to haunt us.

"No," she said sharply, "it's a giant *sucker* they put up just in your honor."

"You know," I said, trying to sound like Mom and keep my spirits up, "this moving is hard enough without you being nasty on top of it all."

Betsy stepped back and put her hands on her hips. "I've been thinking about what Dad said, and you *should* worry about making friends," she said directly. "You are a *boy*. And boys don't make friends, just enemies. Girls make friends like this," she said, snapping her fingers. "Boys just size each other up like hungry wolves fighting over a hunk of red meat. And believe me," she said, poking me in my soft belly, "you'll make a nice meal for someone."

Just then Mom walked up to us. "That Gulf sign makes us look like we have jaundice," she said, holding me by the chin and looking into my eyes. "Even your eyeballs are orange." She pulled down the shade, then looked at Betsy and put her arm around her shoulders. "Come on," she said warmly, "help me make up the beds and get this place organized."

"Okay," Betsy said. She sounded tired of being miserable.

"Jack! Pete!" Dad called from the front door. "Come help me unload the trunk."

"Yes, sir!" I hollered back, and saluted in his direction.

"Yes, sir!" Pete said, and crawled off the couch. He was tired of being miserable, too.

After Mom got the kitchen boxes unpacked, we ate dinner from the cooler full of leftover food we had packed for the trip. As I looked around the table, it seemed that everyone was doing much better. Betsy was happy because she had gotten her own little room. As usual, I had to share with Pete. Mom was happy because the house was clean and easy to keep that way. And Dad looked ready to hit the sack and get charged up for his new *ambitious* life.

After I took a shower in something like a tin phone booth, I said good night to everyone and crawled between my sheets, which smelled like Cream of Wheat. I was exhausted, but before I fell asleep I still wondered what the kids at school might want to hear about me. I knew Mom was right, that I should just tell the simple truth: I was from a small farm town full of nice people with enough oddballs thrown in to make the place interesting. But I was more attracted to Dad's advice. It just seemed much more fun to make up who I was, to invent myself so everyone would think I was interesting. And suddenly it struck me that maybe Dad said to tell people what they want to hear because he knew life was easier that way, that if you agreed with everyone they wouldn't say mean things about you, or pick on you. I wanted to get up and ask him if that's what he meant by telling people what they wanted to hear, but I knew he was already asleep, and wouldn't want to hear from me. Soon, I didn't want to hear from myself anymore and drifted into sleep.

In the morning I opened my eyes and looked directly out my window. There was a kid staring at me. He was standing up to his knees in the little swamp between our two trailer homes. His hair formed a perfect V down the middle of his forehead, kind of like the pointy end of a can opener or, as Dad would say, a church key. When he saw me staring back at him he waved.

"Where are you from-from-from?" he asked, sloshing through the pea-green water.

"New York City," I replied, lying before I could stop myself. I guess I was more Dad than Mom.

"Oh," he said, impressed. "We're from a town so small-small-small I'm sure you've never heard of it. My dad's a carpenter for the Seabees."

"My dad's an admiral," I said, lying through my teeth. I couldn't seem to help myself, then I lied some more. "But he's wearing a disguise so he can catch all the *un*ambitious sailors who just goof off all day."

The kid looked back at me with his head bobbing up and down like a dog toy in the back window of a car. "Wow, I always wanted to meet an admiral's kid," he said. "Do you ever get to steer the ships?"

"Steer them, *and* fire off the big guns," I boasted.

His jaw dropped. "What's your-your-your name?" he asked, repeating his words like the excited goose in *Charlotte's Web*.

"Jackson," I said, "like President Jackson." I knew I was off to a bad start. "What's yours?"

"Julian," he replied, splashing forward and up onto dry ground until he could stick his wet hand through my window.

I shook it. "Nice to meet you," I said. At least that wasn't a lie.

I found the little mirror on the way home from school. It was propped up in the grass by the side of the road and as I walked by the sun shined down at just the right angle and the reflection zapped me straight in the eye. It got me good, like a bee had stung me on the tip of my eyeball. I jerked my head to one side and circled around behind it as if I were sneaking up on a poisonous snake. I reached down and picked it up. It was pretty cool because it must have come off an old car and was a big hunk of chrome with a mirror in the middle. As soon as I got it in my hands I began to reflect the light around as if it were a laser beam. Immediately

I knew that in my hands it would be a lot of trouble. Farther off to the side of the road was a line of sand dunes and tall grass. It was the perfect sniper's nest. I ran up the dune and flopped down on the other side. My first victim was on a bicycle. He looked like he was in second grade. Wh

yards a thirty
in the. right
his eyes shielded

, while the other tried to steer. I zapped him again and ducked. I could hear the bike hit the ground. "Oww!" the kid yelled then got up and pedaled away with a clank! clank! clank! where his chain guard was off center.

I knew the mirror was trouble in my hands and I should just go throw it into the ocean, but I did not. Instead I zapped a few drivers and watched them squint and shield their eyes as they drove by. Then, one of them stopped, badly. He hit the brakes and there was sand on the road and he did a one-eighty. When the guy got out of his car I stood up in a panic and ran. He ran after me and hollered, "I'll get you, you scrawny little nitwit."

I ran toward the surf and waded into the water. When I was waist deep I threw the mirror as far as I could. I was lucky the guy was in good clothes and didn't come after me.

The water receded, the sky cleared, school began, and I was in luck. My new teacher was young and enthusiastic and full of great creative ideas. Each morning she dashed through the classroom door with her long wet hair smelling like a bouquet of flowers and her arms filled with papers and supplies for projects. "Sorry, I just got out of the shower," she'd say breathlessly as she dumped everything on her desk then flicked the blond strands of hair out of her blue eyes. She was smart. She was beautiful. I loved her instantly.

My third-grade teacher back in Pennsylvania was old and worn-out. It had been her last year before retirement and instead of treating us like students, she turned us into her own private staff of servants. When she pulled up in the parking lot, we hustled out to her car and carried in all her book bags, her purse, her special low-salt lunch, her favorite pillow, and her embroidery kit. Then we gently supported her shaky arms as we took baby steps all the way inside to her desk. Her hair was as dried out as steel wool. She was rusting away and spent no time thinking about how to make education fun. Instead, she always gave us plain old workbook assignments after settling down in her chair for the day. She had a large alarm clock ticking loudly on her desk, and it regularly went off with an ear-drilling ring whenever she needed to take one of her many medications. Because of her age and ailments she was excused from cafeteria duty, and after lunch we would creep back into the classroom to find her slumped forward on her desk napping with her head on an unfinished embroidered pillow. We'd pull the curtains and turn off the lights and she'd sleep until the alarm clock rang. She'd wake up confused and stare out at us with eyeballs as murky as peeled grapes. She seemed not to know where she was. It was like having class in a very sad retirement home. For extra credit we could rub her feet. She had corns and bunions that were as big as the knobs on an old radio. She gave us a tool that looked something like a cheese grater and we scratched it back and forth over the knobs and shaved them down a bit like you would a radish. At the end of the year we chipped in and bought her an automatic foot massager.

But my new teacher was like a college girl. I stared up at her dreamily all day long and did everything she asked. And when she needed a volunteer I alertly raised my hand before I even knew what she required. If she had said, "I need a body to dissect," I would have thrown myself across her desk with a scalpel between my teeth. I dreamed she would carve her initials into my shoulder. If she needed a kidney I'd donate one of mine. In a very rare operation we could switch beating hearts. She called on me a lot, and I was certain she thought I was the special one in class, even though my mind drifted a bit.

After about a week Miss Noelle stood thoughtfully in front of us and slowly rolled up her shirtsleeves. She looked us up and down one by one, as if we were slabs of stone she was about to carve. "I have a great desire to get to know you all better," she announced. "So I've come up with a fun writing assignment. First, I want each of you to write the story of your life exactly as it is. No exaggerations. No stretching the truth. Then, I want you to write a second biography which is the story of your life as you *wish* it to be."

I loved the idea. She was so *inventive*.

"I need a volunteer," she called out.

Reflexively my hand shot up, and without hesitation she called on me. "Pass out one of these composition books to every student," she instructed. "They'll be your *ungraded*, write-whatever-you-want journals. Anything goes! Shoot for the moon!"

I leaped out of my seat and grabbed a stack of black-and-white composition books off her desk. I passed them out with my head held high as if I were a priest delivering communion.

Soon, we all picked up our pens and bent our heads and got busy. It didn't take long to write the basics of my real life—where I was born, the names of my family members, and the few exciting things that had happened to me—all written in detail just as honestly as my mom would have told it.

But when it came to writing about my life as I wished it would be, I found it a bit more difficult because I could hear my dad's voice in the back of my head saying, "Tell her what she wants to hear." I just didn't know yet if she wanted to hear that I was madly in love with her.

I was sucking on the tip of my pen and turning my tongue blue when over the loudspeaker the secretary's voice burst in. "Excuse me, Miss Noelle. Could you send Jack Henry down to the principal's office?"

I glanced over at Miss Noelle with an alarmed look on my face.

She winked at me, then nodded toward the classroom door. "Chin up," she said.

But as I meandered down to the principal's office I was nervous. The office secretary spotted the panicky look on my face. "Don't worry," she assured me. "Mrs.

Nivlash won't bite. She's simply lovely." I had been bitten by a lot of lovely dogs that were not supposed to bite. As the secretary opened the principal's office door she announced my name and with her hip nudged me forward.

Mrs. Nivlash was wearing a bright yellow suit that my mom would describe as a businesswoman's *mannish* suit. She had been out in the sun a lot. She looked like well-dressed beef jerky. An orange scarf twisted around her neck gave her shiny face a devilish glow. I squinted at her as if looking into a ring of fire.

"I've been meaning to take this opportunity to welcome you to our school," she said politely, dipping a tea bag into a cup of steaming water. She stood and leaned across her desk to shake. Her hand was large and her fingers wrapped around my palm and wrist like bony cables. "Take a seat," she said, releasing her grip. I tipped back into a chair. "I've been thinking that your arrival at First Flight Elementary is a great opportunity for all of us, because we have a problem here and I think a new boy like you can help." She fished the tea bag out of the cup and squeezed it dry. "Let me explain. Last year there was a horrendously bad gum-chewing epidemic going on around campus. Just awful. Gum was stuck everywhere, to everything. Over the summer we had to pay out a lot of money to have the gum professionally removed. And this year, I don't want it to get started again. So here's what I plan to do, and here is where *you* fit in. I'm going to make a new school service position—we have a head of safety patrol, and a head of school spirit, and a head of academic excellence. And now I'm going to give you the title of Respect Detective. You will be the head of school respect. What do you think of that?"

With her little finger she dabbed at the caked red lipstick in the corners of her mouth, then paused. I wasn't sure what she wanted from me. I tried to look into her eyes for a clue, but when I did mine slid away from hers as if our eyes were opposing magnets. I glanced around her office to see if I could gather any hints. Her bookshelves were lined with detective novels. She had a target-shooting trophy in the shape of an enormous golden pistol. Her letter opener looked like a bayonet. There was a framed photograph of her dressed as a police officer. All I could assume was that she had had a previous career in law enforcement before deciding to run a school. Perhaps, she figured, if she could set straight the up-and-coming criminals when they were young, it was better than catching them after they had committed some awful crimes as adults. That made sense to me.

Mrs. Nivlash cleared her throat. "Well?" she asked.

Her hands gripped and twisted and ungripped each

other like competing wrestlers. I could tell she was a person who didn't like to be disappointed. In this case I knew it was better to follow Dad's rule and tell her exactly what she wanted to hear.

"I'm very excited," I said, as respectfully as possible. "Very."

"Good," she said warmly, then stood up and closed her door. When she sat down again she smiled gleefully and leaned toward me. "Now here's the plan. I'm going to allow gum chewing for a one-week trial period. If they're good, I'll promise to extend it for another week but, believe me, it won't get that far. Now, you may think it is mighty strange that a principal would allow gum chewing, but there is a method to my madness. I'm guessing that our little gum-sticking criminal will not resist the first opportunity to stick his or her gum where it does not belong, and this is where you come in. As the newly created Respect Detective, you will be my eyes and ears among the students. You will identify the gum sticker, and you will turn him in to me. In return," she said slowly, pointing her finger directly into my face, "I will take very good care of you. Unless you do something bad yourself, I will see to it that nobody troubles you. Any questions?"

"Well, what if nobody sticks gum on things?"

She threw her head back and laughed so hard she

snorted. "Impossible!" she said when she had settled down. "We're dealing with *kids*. Give them any little chance to screw things up and they will."

She unlocked a file-cabinet drawer beneath her desk, opened it, and removed a manila folder clearly marked SECRET in red ink. She flipped it open and set aside a Respect Detective identification card. "Here," she said after writing my name on it. "I had this made up for your new position."

"Should I pin it on my shirt?" I asked.

"Heavens no," she said sharply. "It's just between us. Keep it hidden. Don't let anyone see it. Not even the teachers. They chew gum, too."

"Okay," I said, and shoved it down into my back pocket.

"Now get going," she instructed. "I'll make the gum-chewing announcement today. Then I want you to keep your eyes open for the perpetrator."

"What will you do when you catch him?" I asked.

"I'll make him the new Respect Detective," she said, smiling broadly. "I think it will be rehabilitative for each perpetrator to have to catch the next violator."

How clever, I thought. No wonder she was the principal.

When I left her office I was so relieved I wasn't in trouble that I didn't think a lot about what it meant to be her Respect Detective. I shrugged it off as one of those weird yearbook categories like Dress-Code Coordinator or Manners Monitor. I was mostly thinking about Miss Noelle and getting back to the class so I could dream about our perfect life together and occasionally do a little work on the writing assignment.

By recess I still hadn't written anything about what I wished for, because I wasn't quite sure Miss Noelle and I were thinking alike. I sat in the shade under the sliding board and simply wished that somehow we lived together, that she was my teacher, my mom, my big sister, and my girlfriend rolled into one. I wished we lived on a yacht. I wished we were CIA spies. I wished we were on game shows together and won sensational vacation trips and stacks of cash. All my wishing was confusing and made me blush when just thinking about nothing more than holding her hand. So I tried not to think about it, and I certainly couldn't write about it, because what I had in mind was so disrespectful I'd have to turn myself in to Mrs. Nivlash.

Suddenly the gym teacher blew his chrome whistle. Our heads snapped around toward him. "Everyone off the playground and back to your classrooms!" he instructed, waving toward the side entrance. "Now!" he barked, as if a cloud of enraged killer bees were swarming toward us. We froze for a second, then followed his orders. He was young and energetic and wore tight white T-shirts to show off his muscles. I didn't like him because he was always poking his sunburned nose into our classroom and asking Miss Noelle if she needed help disciplining any of the boys or had time after school for some extra tutoring. Some kid told me he had been a pro football player who had received a terrible career-ending injury. Whatever the injury was, I couldn't locate it. Perhaps it was deep inside his head. As my dad would say, "Too many games without a helmet."

On my way back toward the building I looked over my shoulder and saw why recess was being cut short. A row of black limousines, lined up like a chain of fallen dominoes, slowly pulled to a halt along the street. I knew it wasn't the president coming to visit our school because all the cars had small purple-and-white flags flying from their front fenders. Their headlights were on. It was a funeral procession. Our playground was separated by a chain-link fence from the cemetery I'd seen that first night in Cape Hatteras. The school had an agreement with the cemetery that during a weekday burial service all the schoolkids would be called inside rather than be allowed to hang over the fence and point and gawk at the polished casket and the family members looking as sad and crumpled as balled-up laundry.

Just then I spotted Mrs. Nivlash at her office window. She held a pair of binoculars to her eyes and scanned the playground and funeral. That's right, I reminded myself, I'm the Respect Detective. I'd better get busy. I dutifully checked the playground to make certain all the kids were respectful. A few kids had stopped running for the door and had turned back to point at the limousines. They craned their necks and jumped up and down to get a better look at the casket. Just when I thought I might have to turn them in to Mrs. Nivlash, the gym teacher blew his whistle and threatened to jab their eyes out with a red-hot needle if they didn't get a move on. They bolted for the door.

After we filed back into the school and returned to our seats, I raised my hand. "Miss Noelle," I said after she called on me, "I'm having trouble with the assignment. It's easy to write about my life as it really is, but I'm kind of stuck on writing about the life I wish for."

She smiled. "You mean to tell me you don't know what to *wish* for in life?" She crossed her hands over her heart and made a cheerless, turned-down-mouth clown face. "That is heartbreaking," she whimpered with mock despair. Behind me there were a few laughs.

Suddenly I felt panicked inside and realized that to her, and to others, I must have appeared shamefully pathetic. But I wasn't pathetic—my wish was just too personal to share.

"Don't get all bogged down in reality," she said, snapping out of her act. "Let your imagination run wild. Cut loose. Think of what a wonderful life it would be if you could get everything you wanted. Or if you could be great at everything you attempted. Be smarter, wiser, bigger, more clever . . . more handsome . . ."

My cheeks and ears reddened. I could hear a few more snickers behind me but then I was saved when Mrs. Nivlash's voice flooded the room. "Good afternoon, students and staff," she announced. "I just want to wish you all a great school year and, to kick it off, I have decided to allow you a privilege unheard of in any other school across America. I am allowing you to chew gum."

Our class let out a cheer, and down the hall I could hear the echoes of the other cheering classrooms full of kids. My heart began to pound. Slowly I looked around the room. Everyone was thrilled. They were all talking about gum. Chewing gum. Buying gum. Swapping gum. Bubble gum. Hot gum. Licorice gum.

"But of course," continued Mrs. Nivlash as her voice rose, "this is a privilege that must be constantly earned. So if you are respectful of the school and dispose of your gum properly, then you may continue to enjoy the privilege for the entire year. *But* if I find one piece of gum stuck anywhere, then the privilege will be revoked. I know many of you think that when I'm not looking you can stick it wherever you wish, but watch yourself. I have appointed a student Respect Detective who will secretly be my eyes and ears among you—and he'll be watching. So, enjoy your privilege and I look forward to a great year."

"I wonder who the snitch is?" I heard one kid ask another.

"I don't know," he replied roughly, and pounded his fist into his open hand. "But my dad always says, 'The only good snitch is a *dead* snitch.'"

Suddenly I began to get the creepy feeling that being the Respect Detective was not going to be appreciated by the other kids.

And I felt worse once I returned home. Betsy was in the kitchen eating an avocado half-filled with wine vinegar. It was her favorite snack and made her breath so acidic she could melt the head off a toothbrush.

"Can I ask your advice about something?" I asked timidly.

"Sure," she replied and spooned a curl of avocado out of its shell, slipped it into her mouth, then washed it down with a sip of vinegar.

I told her about being named Mrs. Nivlash's Respect Detective. "Do you think it's a good thing or a bad thing?" I asked. "I'm a little confused."

She looked at me as if I were a complete idiot. "Naming you the Respect Detective is just a scam," she said. "What you really are is her head spy. Her mole, tattletale, stool pigeon, snake in the grass . . . Now do you get it? She has set you up to be her *rat*. And when everyone finds out, they'll do what is always done to rats—they'll corner you and crush you to death with giant stones."

Tombstones, I thought. They'll use bloodhounds to track me down in the cemetery, then push me into an open grave and do me in. The air went slowly out of my lungs as if it were my last breath. "That's what I'm afraid of," I said with a shudder.

She took another sip of vinegar and screwed up her face. When she smacked her lips it sounded like a whip snapping. "You are really up to your neck in it this time," she continued.

"How can I get out of this?" I pleaded.

"Who do you want to hate you the most—Mrs. Nivlash or the students?"

"I don't want anyone to hate me," I said, already hating myself for being stupid.

"Too late for that," she said. "But I'm warning you, if the other kids find out you are a snitch you are going to have to enter the witness protection program."

That night I lay in bed looking out my window and over the little swamp. I felt like pond scum. No amount of wishing would get me out of the jam I was in. Even my favorite time-wasting activity of dreaming about Miss Noelle was now ruined. All I could think about was being Mrs. Nivlash's dead rat. It was awful.

The next morning I passed by the cemetery on my

way to school. I could see the new grave with its silvery granite tombstone. A few rows away a backhoe was clawing at the sand, preparing for another coffin. "That will be me," I whispered to myself, "if I don't get out of this mess." By the time I opened the front door, I knew what I had to do. Instead of going to class, I went directly into the front office. I pulled the secretary to one side. "I need to speak to the principal," I whispered. "Top secret."

In a minute I was in Mrs. Nivlash's office. When she saw me she smiled, but not for long.

"I don't think I'm cut out for this job," I said to her, and held out my Respect Detective identification card.

"Why?" she asked, and stared hard into my face. I looked down at her hands. Her fingers wiggled about like the desperate legs on an overturned crab.

"It takes too much time away from class," I said, lying. "I don't spend as much time thinking about my teacher as I should."

She smiled down at me. "How do you like your nice, *pretty* teacher?" she asked in a syrupy voice.

"I *love* her," I blurted out. "She's the best."

"Well, I might have to transfer you to another class," she continued, amused with herself. "You get my drift?"

I got it. "Okay," I said, backing off. "I'll stick with the job."

"Smart boy," Mrs. Nivlash replied, smiling brightly. "Now get busy."

I did. I ran out of the office and down to my class-room and threw myself into my seat. I took a deep breath, then suddenly realized I was in deeper trouble than I had feared. *Everyone* had gum. The class sounded like a herd of cows chewing and smacking and snap-ping. The air was sweet from the smell of grape and cherry and strawberry and clove and mint. I was sur-rounded.

I put my face down on my desk. Somewhere, an overblown bubble popped. That's going to be my head, I thought, once Mrs. Nivlash sees this. Suddenly a fin-ger poked me on the shoulder.

I bolted straight up in my seat. "Arghhh!" I cried out.

"Sorry," the kid behind me said. "I thought you might like a bubble-gum cigar. I brought a whole pack."

"No, thanks," I said breathlessly. "I can't chew it. My dad's a dentist. He forbids us to have gum. He checks my breath after school."

"I have some trick gum," he replied, reaching into his top pocket. "It tastes just like bad breath."

"I have to go to the bathroom," I said suddenly. I jumped up and fled for the door. As I dashed down the hallway I scanned the floor and walls for gum. There was none on the light switches or fire alarm pulls. I went inside the boys' room. None on the floor. I looked in the stalls. I checked the toilet seats. They were dis-gusting, but no gum. I ran out. I passed the water fountain. No gum on the mouth guard, or in the drain, or on the handle. I ran to the next bathroom. No gum. I passed the library. The librarian, Mrs. Alice, defied Mrs. Nivlash with a sign reading: STILL NO GUM ALLOWED. I gave her the thumbs up as I dashed by. There was nothing in the lost and found. By the time I made it back to class, Miss Noelle had arrived. "Okay, students," she was saying. "Put the gum away and take out your journals." Quickly I threw a penny on the floor and got down on my hands and knees to search for it. I didn't care about the penny. I was looking up at the undersides of everyone's desks to make certain no one had parked a wad of gum there.

"Jack," Miss Noelle said sharply, "what are you doing crawling around on all fours?"

I jumped up so fast I got dizzy. My knees buckled and I stumbled around like a drunk while the room turned into a silent black-and-white film, then back to normal.

"Are you sick?" she asked. "Do you need to see the nurse?"

"Yes," I said. I grabbed my book bag and as I left the room my head twitched wildly as my eyes jerked around, searching for signs of improperly discarded gum.

In the nurse's office I told her I had the flu. She laid me out on the uncomfortable plastic-covered bed and slipped a thermometer under my tongue, then went back to reading a book on flesh-eating infectious diseases. To calm down I lay there and thought only of Miss Noelle. If I lived at her house, I could help her think up clever assignments. I could help her grade papers. After school I'd help her redo the hallway bulletin boards. My desk would be directly next to hers. We would think up little codes and signals so we could communicate privately in front of the students. We'd pass snappy notes back and forth, and smile knowingly into each other's eyes. Just imagining this totally fulfilling life made me purr like a relaxed cat.

Suddenly the nurse removed the thermometer and squinted at it. She scowled and gave it a shake. "You're fine," she declared.

I knew better. I was sick in a way no thermometer could detect.

After school I passed the cemetery. I had the idea to go in and find a quiet spot to sit and think about my imaginary life, because I knew that once I got home my *real* life would take over and I'd have no time to myself. I walked in and looked around. The rows of tombstones looked like giant toes sticking out of the ground. I walked over to where the last person had been buried and examined the fresh dirt piled up on the grave. Large bouquets of flowers were spread around the stone. Some of them were on tripods, with the stems woven into circular wreaths big enough to fit around the head of a horse. I lifted one and stuck my head through the middle. I tried to imagine the circle as a life preserver, but it read REST IN PEACE in black ribbon.

The cemetery must have influenced my imagination. I suddenly imagined myself trapped by the students, who wrapped me up in a ball of stringy gum and left me to rot to death like a bug caught in a spider's web. At the funeral Miss Noelle would kneel down on my burial mound and weep. "I'll never love another," she'd whimper.

I didn't write all this down because it was warped and I didn't think she wanted to hear it. I figured what I was imagining would scare her. My own dream life made me feel weird and nervous, and it confused me that picturing my own death made me happier. I thought I might need a doctor. I hopped up. From where I was, I could see across the cemetery and school playground over to the teachers' parking lot. There was Miss Noelle walking toward her car and by her side was the muscle-bound gym teacher. She opened her car door, they said a few things, then he leaned over and kissed her on the cheek. That was definitely not part of my dream. I felt weak. Maybe it was a mirage? Maybe my mind was playing tricks on me? I staggered out of the cemetery as stunned as Lazarus must have felt after he rose from the dead.

———

I stayed in my room for the rest of the day. I didn't eat dinner and I didn't sleep well. In the morning I inched my way to school. Miss Noelle was full of enthusiasm as we began to share our "wished-for lives" in class. Most everyone was pretty straightforward as they read from their journals. There were five teachers, two presidents, a pirate, three rock stars, a great white shark, a fashion model, a veterinarian, an admiral, a fireman, a chef, and then it was my turn.

"Jack," Miss Noelle said sweetly, "I saved you for last. Now would you please share your wish with us."

I just knew she was waiting for me to say something wildly imaginative. But I couldn't. I hadn't written a word. "Can I go to the bathroom first?" I asked.

"Hurry back," she said, glancing up at the clock. "We have other subjects to cover today."

I ran for the door and down the hall. Once again I checked the hallway floor. No gum. The walls. The water fountain. The toilets. No gum. I took a quick sprint through the cafeteria and glanced under the tables. My heart stopped! There was a piece. As I reached out to remove it, Mrs. Nivlash came around the corner. I didn't want her to think I was sticking it there so I quickly unstuck it, popped it into my mouth, and began to chew. It was crunchy with some hard cereal crumbs mixed in with it. I waved to her as I ran off. I used a shortcut back through the gym, spit the gum into a trash can, and with a final burst of speed ran outside and checked the bus drop-off spots. It was all clean.

By the time I returned to class, Miss Noelle was working on math.

"Sorry that took so long," I said, and rubbed my belly as if I'd had a problem. "I'll lead off next time."

She raised an eyebrow when she looked at me, and I knew she wasn't going to let me off the hook so easily.

For the rest of the day Miss Noelle treated me like a regular kid. She only looked my way occasionally. When I volunteered for snack duty, she called on someone else. I knew she was annoyed with me for letting her down, and before long I began to imagine the punishments she would give me. I'd have to wash the blackboards. Alphabetize her books. Water the plants. Clean the hamster cage. I was ready for punishment. I felt I needed it. It wasn't right to have a *crush* on my teacher. It was unhealthy. Weird. I just didn't know what to do about it. Should I tell her? Or not?

Then just before the bell rang she said, "Jack, could you stay behind after class?"

"Yes," I replied, feeling nervous as a cricket as I sat there scratching at myself and waiting for the room to empty.

When we were alone, Miss Noelle sat sideways in the desk next to mine. "I'm still waiting to hear about your life as you wish it to be," she said.

"I wish I could give it to you," I replied. "But every-thing I wish for seems so wrong."

"How can a wish be wrong?" she asked.

"Trust me," I said. "I wish for all the wrong things."

"Tell me," she said. "Give me an example."

"What would you like to hear?" I asked.

"Whatever," she said, and shrugged. "I'm open."

"No, you tell me what you want to hear, and then I'll wish for it," I said.

"You've got it all wrong," she said. "You wish first."

"No," I said. "I want my wish to add up to what you want, then my wish will come true."

She sighed. "That's not how a wish works," she said. "Your wishes are just wild, crazy desires. They don't have to come true."

"Yes, they do," I insisted. "How can you wish for something if there is no chance it will come true?"

She put her hand on my shoulder and gave it a squeeze that was like half a wish coming true. "Do you mind if I make a wish?" she asked.

"Sure, go ahead," I said.

"I wish you'd just tell me what it is you aren't writ-ing."

I took a deep breath. It was time to tell her. I couldn't get through a whole year feeling like this without being a nervous wreck each day. "I have a crush on you," I whispered, and felt all the blood in my body gather in my face, which heated up like a hot plate. My head tilted forward from the weight. I felt faint.

"Well, everyone's had a crush on a teacher at one time or another," she said. "I had several. I'm sure you will have others, too, and on it goes. It's natural, enjoy it."

"I'm trying to," I croaked, but I had a cramp in my foot and I was sweating and still blushing so dangerously that I thought my head might burst into segments like an overripe tomato.

"I think some of the best friendships start with a crush. Don't you?"

"I-I don't know," I stammered. "I'm still at the crush stage."

"Trust me," she said. "You'll move on. Once you see me for who I am, you'll be happy we're just friends."

"Okay," I said, wanting the conversation to end.

"Do you have any other wishes?"

"There was one where I died."

"That was your wish?" she asked, alarmed. "To die?"

"Among others," I said.

"Are you okay?" she asked. "I mean, sick or depressed—things at home a little difficult?"

"No," I said, "nothing like that. Really. I'm very happy. I didn't want to die, but I knew you couldn't have a crush on me because you have one on the gym teacher. So I was settling for your *pity*."

She threw her arms up into the air. "No more pity!" she cried. "Stop it. Nothing could be more of a *turnoff* than pity."

"Oh," I said. "How do you know?"

"The gym teacher," she said in a whisper. "He was supposed to be an NFL star and got hurt and all he wants now is *pity, pity, pity*. Well, I have no wish to be locked up like a *pity* princess in his *pity* palace. Yuck."

I smiled. That was good news.

"So no more of this pity stuff," she said. "Let's just have a great relationship and a great year. Deal?"

"Deal," I said. I stuck out my hand and we shook. "Nice hand," I said.

"You're weird," she replied.

Already it felt like a friendship.

That night I wrote in my school journal about my life as I wished it would be—which I imagined was the life that Miss Noelle was already living. "I wish for the ability to always see the good things in life instead of all the bad things. This would make me happier than anything else I can think of."

Then, on a separate sheet of paper, I made a list of all the good, respectful things I had seen at First Flight Elementary. After that, I slept really well.

Too well. I woke up late. I dressed quickly and was trotting along the sandy side of the road when Miss

Noelle zipped by. She saw me and slammed on her brakes. "Hey, buddy," she called out, "need a ride?"

"Sure," I said. I opened the car door, cleared about a million things off her front seat, and hopped in.

"How's the crush doing?" she asked.

I looked over at her. Her long blond hair was wet and the wind was blowing it around. She was smiling and her eyes seemed full of the clever ideas she had been up thinking about all night. "I think the friendship part is beginning to take hold," I said.

"Great," she replied. "I told you it would. Now, are you ready to read your life story as you wish it to be?"

"Definitely," I said.

She parked the car and hustled off to the teacher's workroom to copy some project material. "Meet you in class," she hollered, like an old friend.

But before I got to class Mrs. Nivlash pulled me aside with one of her strong hands and led me into her office. "What have you found out?" she asked. "I'm desperate to get all the dirt on everyone."

I may have told Miss Noelle the truth, but I was definitely going to keep telling Mrs. Nivlash what I thought she really needed to hear.

"This is a great school," I said. "I've always heard that behind every well-run school is a fantastic principal."

"Oh, for goodness' sake," she groaned, and slapped her desk. A few papers fluttered off the edge. "Tell me

what you know before you smell up the room with another load of bull."

She sounded exactly like my dad, and like him, I
knew there was one thing that would wear her down.
Niceness. After all, he had married my mom and she
was the nicest person I knew.

I gave her my list of all the kids who I had seen do
something nice—kids who had stopped playground
fights, who had helped teachers carry books, kids who
had been kind to the senior-citizen volunteers, who had
shared at lunch, who had helped younger kids with
reading, who had picked up trash, who had taken
turns—it was a long list.

"This isn't what I'm looking for," she said, frowning.
"I want the dirt. Not the nice stuff."

"But don't you think that by pointing out the good
things nice kids do, you'll send a message through the
whole school that nice kids are who you respect? And
that bad kids are not what you are looking for all the
time? Maybe bad kids will get the message and be like
the good kids."

"That's one way of looking at it," she said. "But I find
it more satisfying to catch the corrupt."

"And one final thing," I said, "about the gum." I
pulled a piece of folded paper out of my pocket and
passed it to her. I had written the gym teacher's name
on it. She opened it and read it, and looked at me with

one eyebrow raised in suspicion, or maybe she had sus-
pected him all along. "You didn't hear it from me," I
whispered. I put the Respect Detective ID card on her
desk, turned, and smiled as I headed for the door. As I
walked down the hall I crammed two pieces of Dubble
Bubble into my mouth, and by the time I stuck it to the
gym teacher's door I had chewed all the sugar out of it.

That afternoon we were reading limericks when Mrs.
Nivlash's voice came over the loudspeaker. "I want to
say how proud of everyone I am for behaving so respectfully this week . . ." Then she went on to praise the
behavior of the kids who were nice, who were thought-
ful, helpful, well mannered, polite, brave, honest, car-
ing, and kind to others. And as she called out the names
of the good kids, I looked around the classroom. I could
tell that everyone was *wishing* their names would be
called.

Wasted Space

I was in the kitchen watching Betsy make cookies. I was like a dog lurking around, hoping for scraps. First, she rolled out the cookie dough into a flat sheet. Then she took cookie cutters and cut the dough into a dozen anchor and star shapes. Then she pulled up the rest of the cookie dough. It sagged from where the dough had been cut out. Then suddenly she balled it up and tossed it into the garbage.

"What are you doing?" I asked.

"Throwing away the leftovers,"

she said.

"But that's good dough," I said. "Don't waste it."

"It's no good," she said. "It's waste."

"Nothing is ever wasted," I said.

"Not so," she said. "Take a good look in the mirror. You are a waste of good air."

"Not s—" I even _____ hing, ____ me Thing." ___ me snot back.

"Give me an example,"

I paused for a moment and I couldn't think of anything smart or clever. "I don't know right now," I said, "But I will someday. I just have to believe that nothing done is ever wasted otherwise there is more thrown away and useless

in the world than used and
good."

"That's the difference between us,"
said Betsy. "I sort out the good from
the bad in life and you just
drift around in a pretty pink
bubble all day."

I went to my bedroom to
get away from her. She was so
negative. I started thinking
about what was positive. I liked
reading. That wasn't a waste
although Dad said I sit on my
butt all day. I liked looking
out the window as if the view
were a movie even though Mom
said I needed to pay attention
more. I liked taking long walks
on the beach even if I didn't
find a shell. That kind of thinking

One day after a few weeks of building new officers' quarters for the Navy brass, Dad came home disgusted. Mom was grocery shopping with Pete and Betsy. When she was around he'd watch his tongue and house manners. But when she was out of the house Dad felt unleashed to say and do anything he wanted. He could curse, belch, and put his feet up on the coffee table with his sandy work boots still on. He could spit in the sink, pee without lifting the toilet seat, and wipe his hands on the back of his pants. And now that he had overheated and blown his fuse, I was the only one at home to hear him out.

"You know," he started up, flipping his dirty bucket cap toward the arm of the couch. He missed. It hit the floor and slid into the corner where it looked like a dog bowl. "The last time I was in the Navy I was a kid and it was a lot easier to take orders from the upper ranks. But I'm older now and my so-called superior officers are not looking so *superior*. They may outrank me, but they can't outthink me."

I didn't argue with him when he was down in the dumps. Instead, I took a page out of Mom's book and said, "I'm sure you are a lot smarter than the ranking officers. They must be pretty dumb not to listen to you." This was exactly what she would say. In spite of what she might think, Mom always knew what *he* wanted to hear.

He yanked open the refrigerator and pulled out a can of beer. He popped it with an opener and a hissing geyser of suds shot up. Dad jumped back as if a snake had bitten him, then he leaned over the sink and blew the foam into the drain. "I wish Pete would stop shaking up the beer," he barked. "That kid is turning into a menace." He gave me a look as if I had taught Pete how to be a pain in his neck.

Then his shoulders slumped and he got down on himself. "Maybe I'm not as smart as I think I am," he muttered, and slurped up some of the foam. "You know why we are in this mess?" he asked.

I didn't think we were in a mess. I thought we were doing well. My new school was great. We lived in a cam-ouflaged house trailer next to a swamp, our neighbors were fun, and just across the street was the beach. I loved it all, but I kept my mouth shut. It might have been a trick question.

"Bad luck!" he said, answering for me. "Listen to this. Here's how we went broke back home and why I had to rejoin this *rub a dub dub* outfit. I worked for a friend who said he wouldn't let me down, and then he did. I built his bakery—advanced him all the materials and labor—and in the end he refused to pay. He *stiffed* me. Stabbed me in the back. When the bills came I couldn't pay the suppliers and we had to go bankrupt."

"Can't you sue him?" I asked.

"We only made the deal on a handshake," he said glumly. "Just my luck I got ruined by a friend, someone I trusted. See what I mean?"

"Yeah," I said, "like it's just my bad luck that Betsy is my sister."

"Hey," he said sharply, and pointed at me, "don't knock your sister. She's smarter than you'll ever be."

I made a mental note to shake up some more of his beer and blame it on Pete.

"I need to turn this mess around," he said. "I lost all my money. I'm losing my patience with the Navy, and my mind is next. After that, there won't be much left of your old man. Seems like it all boils down to luck," Dad said. "I work hard. I do my best. I keep my nose clean, and still I can't get ahead. And I look over at the next guy who does nothing and has a roll of cash in his pocket big enough to choke a horse. *Luck!*" he said, as if he could grab it by the shoulders and give it a shake. "It's about time you roll my way for a change."

"Do you lose sleep over this?" I asked, imitating a psychologist I had seen on TV responding to a patient's complaint that he kept seeing little green gnomes in his rearview mirror.

"The Navy is what I'm losing sleep over," he said. "They're driving me nuts because they figure it is their job to mold me into some kind of mindless swabbie. But it's too late for me. I've already reached the Popeye stage of my life."

"What stage is that?" I asked.

He grinned at me, then tapped on the side of his head. *"I yam what I yam!"* he said, and followed with that *"ga-ga-ga-ga"* Popeye chuckle.

"What's that mean?" I asked.

"It means," said Dad, "like Popeye I am a fully formed adult and *am what I am.* I'm not going to change anymore, so I don't need to worry about being right or wrong all the time. Besides, being right or wrong has nothing to do with getting ahead in life. *Luck* is what a man needs to succeed, and now that I've reached the Popeye stage of life I'm ready to *receive* my share of luck."

He was losing me. I never thought Popeye was that

lucky. Olive Oyl was always flirting with Brutus, and
Sweet Pea was nothing more than a disaster magnet
who gave Popeye heart attacks from trying to keep him
out of harm's way. I got Dad another beer, then retreated to my room before he opened it.

When Mom came home from the store with Pete
and Betsy, she put away some groceries then suddenly
slipped through my doorway and shut the door behind
her. I was busy feeding my tadpoles. I had caught about
a hundred of them in the swamp and kept them lined
up under my window in a row of glass jars I had picked
out of the trash.

"I have to hide something," she whispered.

"What?"

"Your dad's birthday gift."

"What'd you get him?"

"A surf-casting rod like he's been wanting," she said,
smiling because she knew she had gotten him the perfect gift. She also knew that more than wanting one, he
needed one. Every evening around sunset he'd gaze
through the front screened door at the men on the
beach with their twelve-foot-long rods. They'd lean way
back and with both hands cast off overhead as if swat-
ting a piñata, and I could see the glint of light off their
silver spinners and almost hear the singing mosquito
whine of the line as it unwound.

"Did you see that one!" Dad would say excitedly. "I bet he launched that tackle a hundred yards. Boy, that was some cast." At other times he'd call one of us over to watch as a guy reeled in a thick gray fish. "A shark," he said knowingly. "Better to cut the line and lose the hook in its mouth than try to get it out. A shark will play possum on you. Just when you think it's dead and reach down to remove the hook, it'll take off your hand." I stuck mine in my pockets.

Some nights he took a beer and we walked across the street. Up and down the beach I could hear the fishermen warning the strollers, "Casting out!" followed by the swish of the rod slicing through the air and the whine of the line heading out to sea.

"Don't ever stand behind one of those guys when he's casting," Dad warned me. "If the hook catches you, it will sink clean to your bones—or worse."

I imagined a hook catching me in the nose and ripping it off. I'd have to wear a black patch across my gaping nose cavity like a pirate's eye patch. On a good note, my pink nose would turn out to be the perfect bait to catch a prize-winning trophy fish.

"Well, where is the rod?" I asked Mom. It couldn't possibly fit in my tiny room.

"I left it next door at Julian's house," she said. "They slipped it through a crack in their foundation for safekeeping."

"Let's just keep it there," I said. "It won't fit in any room over here."

She frowned. I knew what she was thinking. She didn't want Julian's dad to use it first. We all lived so close together that sometimes things got shared as if we were all one big family. One morning Dad woke up and thought the car had been stolen but it was only Julian's dad who had seen the keys in the ignition and had taken it. He belonged to a band called the Sea Beats and needed to haul his drum set to a dance club. At other times he'd start up our grill and cook hamburgers and hot dogs and never say thanks or offer us some. When he came to visit he always entered the house and took a few steps toward the refrigerator before hollering, "Hello? Anybody home?" I'm sure he hoped we were away so he could help himself.

"Don't worry," I said to Mom. "I'll keep an eye on the hiding place. Besides, Dad's birthday is Saturday so it won't be there long."

She reluctantly agreed. "And I want a theme for this birthday. I want you kids to get him anything related to fishing. You know, tackle and stuff. You probably know more than I do. I've never fished in my life."

I hadn't done much fishing either. But I knew there was a bait-and-tackle shop in Nags Head and I was sure they could sell me something that would help cheer him up.

"I think a birthday bash is just what Dad needs," I said, recalling my earlier conversation with him. "I think he's depressed."

"You're right," she said. "Anytime someone tells him what to do he goes into a decline. But he'll pull out of it and the fishing rod will give him a way to blow off some steam."

"Yeah," I agreed, hoping she was right. Lately he was wound too tight, and that Popeye thing was weird.

On Saturday we had the birthday party and Dad was in a great mood. Mom gave him the surf-casting rod and he about walked on the ceiling. Betsy gave him some silver spinners with triple clusters of glistening hooks. When I saw how menacing they were, I cupped my hand over my nose and took a few steps back. Pete got him a small cooler where he could keep a few cold beers. Once all the oohing and aahing died down, I pulled out my gift. "This is the icing on the cake," I said, and handed it to him. "The universal missing piece."

"I have no idea what you are talking about," he said, as he opened the shoe box I had it wrapped in. He removed the Lucky Buddha. It was carved out of wood and looked like a very fat, very happy Chinese man with his arms raised over his head. The dark wood glowed with something like red shoe polish all over, except for his stomach, where, from constant rubbing, it was down to the raw wood.

"You rub his belly," I said excitedly, "and it will bring you luck."

I was going to get him some fishing tackle but next door to the bait shop was a used furniture and "whatnot" shop. I went in just to look around. I had nothing in mind. Then I saw a lucky horseshoe over the doorway and that reminded me of what Dad really wanted—good luck. The lady wouldn't sell me the horseshoe, but she had something else "even better," she said. That's when she showed me the Buddha. "It's very old and very wise," she informed me in a hushed tone. "The ancients rubbed his belly for luck." I was impressed.

"How'd you come by it?" I asked.

"Unclaimed luggage auction at the customs wharf," she said. "I was lucky."

She sure was. It cost three dollars and I bought it. I also gave him a can of Popeye-brand spinach I found at the grocery store.

Dad set the spinach aside and Mom gave me a screwy look as Dad tried his best to look pleased with the Buddha. "I know you wanted a fishing theme," I said to her, "but really, this is better. I mean, what's a fisherman without some *luck*?"

Dad reached out and rubbed the statue's belly. "O Buddha," he said in a prayerful voice. "God of good fortune, bring on the luck!"

"Jack senior!" Mom said in a mock scolding voice. "Don't be sacrilegious, especially since you haven't been in a church all year."

This only got Dad going even more. He set the Buddha on the dining room table and knelt down on one knee. "O glorious and all-powerful Buddha," he implored like old man Moses on the mountain, "look down on this poor birthday sailor and shower him with good fishing. For this, I beg." He humbly lowered his head.

We all laughed as if Dad's act were a big joke. But deep inside I knew the Buddha was no joke. He was listening. And he would deliver.

It wasn't long before we had eaten our tuna melts and demolished the marlin-shaped cake. Once the paper plates and cups were tossed in the trash and the plastic forks washed, we all crossed the road and climbed over the dunes to watch Dad test out his fishing gear. We stood off to one side as he rigged the pole and got ready to cast. "One second!" I yelled. I had brought the Buddha. "Rub the belly," I said, and held him out. Dad looked over his shoulder to see if anyone was watching. We were alone. He quickly rubbed the belly, then swung his rod all the way back over his shoulder and shouted,

"Casting out!" and let it fly. The silver spinner arced into the air and the reel buzzed as the line unspooled. Finally we saw it hit with a splash. Dad grinned. "I love this!" he sang and did a little dance in the sand. "Love it!" Mom ventured over to his side and he gave her a hug and kiss.

"See," I said to Betsy, "the Buddha is working already."

"Are you a moron?" she asked. "They're married. Of course they hug and kiss. Buddha has nothing to do with anything. Dad might as well have rubbed his beer can."

But I was certain the Buddha was silently working his magic. I *believed* in his power. And I was right.

That evening Julian's dad had gotten the other Seabees together for a birthday poker game. "Just nickel-and-dime stuff," Dad had promised after stepping into the kitchen for a cold one. Before Dad left for the game I held up the Buddha. "Rub the belly," I said.

He rubbed it. "Come on, Buddha," he sang. "Bring lady luck home to Papa!"

"Bet big," I advised him. "You can't lose."

"Sure," he said. "I'll put it all on the line."

Mom gave me a scolding look. I knew she feared that by tomorrow night we'd all be sleeping under the stars with just the clothes on our backs. He'd lost all his money before and she was worried he could do it again.

Betsy stared at me like Medusa trying to turn me into stone. "Don't encourage him," she growled.

"What?" I said innocently, facing them. "What? You just wait. The Buddha will bring us luck. You'll see."

"Right," said Betsy. "And while you're at it why don't you go cut off the foot of a rabbit, catch a leprechaun, and sell your soul to the devil."

A couple of hours later Dad came home and emptied his pockets on the coffee table. There was more than a hundred dollars. "I couldn't lose," he said. "They ran out of money and we had to quit. Where's my new Buddha buddy?"

I had picked a spot of honor for the statue on top of the refrigerator where we could always use some luck. The way we kids were growing, there was a lot of competition for the food. Dad stood up and rubbed the Buddha's belly.

"Keep rubbing," I encouraged. "Maybe you'll get a promotion."

Dad smiled. "Yeah," he said. "It would be great to give orders instead of taking them."

I knew exactly how he felt.

The next day Dad roared up to the house. He jumped out of the car. "Jack!" he hollered. "Hey, Jack!"

From my room I heard him running. I dropped a

tadpole back in its jar and ran toward him. We embraced like children who had been separated at birth.

"That Buddha is remarkable!" he shouted directly into my face while clutching me by the shoulders. "Look at this." He pulled something that looked like a silver dollar out of his pocket. "You know what this is?"

I didn't.

"A piece of eight. Pirate money. Part of Blackbeard's treasure. I found it while cleaning a drainage ditch under the commander's house. It's real treasure."

"Wow," I said. "Can I hold it?"

He flipped it into the air. "Heads you win, tails you win," he said. "It doesn't matter. With the Buddha on our side, we can't lose."

He headed for the refrigerator. He popped open a beer before I could stop him. The spray hit him full force in the face.

"Should've rubbed Buddha's belly first," I said.

The next day he received a letter with a check in it from the guy who had stiffed him. "Unbelievable," Dad said as he flopped back onto the couch. "Betty!" he hollered. "Come in here and see this. You won't believe your eyes."

When Mom read who the check was from, she spun her head around and looked at me. "Where's that Buddha?" she asked.

"He's safe and sound," I said.

Even Betsy was impressed. "Well, let's not wear him out on little stuff. Let's save the luck for something big."

"Like a new bike," Pete pitched in.

"A real house," Mom said.

"Military academy," Betsy said, smiling at me.

"Hold your horses," Dad cautioned. "Let's just take it easy. Jack got me the Buddha for fishing, and it's time to give him a deep-sea workout."

"What will fish ever get us?" Betsy cried out.

"A happy dad and food on the table," he said. "Nothing wrong with that."

"That's right," Mom agreed. She curled her arm around Dad's waist. "You just save your luck for the ocean," she said sweetly. "Maybe you'll pull in a mermaid."

Dad smiled at the thought. "You'd look good with a fish tail," he said, and gave her a peck on the cheek.

I just loved it when they kissed. It cheered me up. It was better than luck. It was better than money. When they were happy it made us all happy, and nothing was better than knowing we belonged together.

The next day after work Dad no longer had to look out the door and watch other people fish. "Jack," he said, "get my fishing gear and the Buddha and let's go across the street for a while."

"Aye-aye, sir," I said, and scrambled to get everything he needed.

"Pete," Dad said gravely as he removed a beer from the refrigerator, "you didn't shake this up, did you?"

"I keep telling you," Pete cried out. "I don't shake the beer."

Dad held the beer can out the kitchen window, took the opener, and popped the top. The suds shot clean into the middle of the swamp. He whistled. "That would have blown my head off," he said. He grabbed an extra one and I followed him outside. He shouldered his rod and reel and I carried the Buddha and tackle box.

When we reached the beach he was eager to get going. Mom had given us only an hour before dinner.

Dad fastened a silver spoon with triple hooks on to the line, then swung back into position with the pole almost parallel to the sand. "Casting out!" he hollered.

"Stop!" I shouted. "Don't forget to rub the Buddha!" I ran toward him with the Buddha held out in front of me like a cross held before a vampire.

But Dad was already in full swing. The hook caught the Buddha under his chin and in an instant launched him out to sea like a stone from a Roman catapult.

"What the heck was that?" Dad shouted.

"Reel him back," I pleaded, jumping up and down. "Reel him in. That was the Buddha!"

Dad was like Popeye after he ate his spinach. He put everything he had into spinning the reel's handle round and round, but it didn't matter. In a minute the silver spoon with the triple hook danced cleanly through the surf and dragged across the sand. I stared at it, horrified, like people in a movie who open their wall safe only to find it empty of all their gold and diamonds. For an instant Dad's expression was the same as mine.

Then he put his hand on my shoulder. "Don't worry," he said. "It's not your fault."

"But you said the Buddha gave you luck."

"I only half-believed it," he said. "The other half of me knew I was just on a lucky roll. It happens."

"How can you be sure?" I asked.

"People wiser than the Buddha know you make your own luck," he said. "If you keep your head down and work hard, luck comes your way sooner or later."

We fished for a while longer. Dad caught a flounder. When he reeled it in I picked it up and worked the hook out of its mouth while it looked up at me with its two odd eyes on one side of its face.

"See," Dad said, "that's a lucky fish. It lay on its side so long its eye drifted around to the other side of his head."

"Dad," I said, "that probably took a hundred million years to evolve."

"Patience," Dad advised. "No patience, no luck."

He was losing me again. Nobody lived to be a hundred million years old.

In the morning I went over to the beach. I walked up and down the shoreline searching for the Buddha as desperately as if I had been washed up on a desert island and I was searching for signs of life. I did find all kinds of cool things—blue sea glass, hollowed-out crabs, an unbroken sand dollar, a size-seven swim fin, and a three-foot-long reef shark. I assumed it was dead, but when I reached down to lift its snout so I could examine its rows of teeth, it still had one bite left. It was just my luck that it got me. Or maybe it was just my luck that I got only seventeen stitches. It wasn't bad. And on the way back home from the Navy clinic Dad put his arm around me and said, "You know, if we hadn't lost our lucky Buddha this never would have happened."

It was nice of him to say that.

Two Green Chairs

One day my mother made an announcement. "I'm going to the store and I'm buying myself a bathing suit." She was all dressed up as if she were going to a fancy party. I had never thought about buying a bathing suit. I always wore a pair of cut-off jeans, or a pair of shorts. Betsy had a suit but I didn't pay much attention to her.

"Have fun," I said to Mom as she got in the car with Dad. He was going to drop her off and pick her up later.

When he came back home he said to me, "no matter what your mother buys tell her it looks great on her."

"Sure," I said.

"You know," he continued, your mother doesn't buy much for herself because she saves money for you kids."

thought of that befo **Romance Novels** winted it our 'or not noticing or befo.

A little while later Dad went to pick her up. As he went out the door he gave me a wink. I was ready to be extra nice.

When they returned I came running up the hall

and before thinking, shouted,
"You look great!"

"Honey," she said, "thanks
but I look the same as I went out."

Then Dad opened the front
door and lugged in a big
green chair. He set it down
in the living room and went
out and got another. After the
two green chairs had been moved
all around the room Mom put
her hands on her hips and
said, "There!"

"Did you get a bathing suit?"
I asked.

"No," she said, "I thought
we needed to spruce up the
house more than sprucing
up me."

I wished she bought the suit.

Being Miss Noelle's *friend* was good for a while, but it was not as satisfying as having a crush on her. As a friend, I could imagine being her equal, as if we were just teaching buddies who shared common interests like windsurfing, or scuba diving through old pirate wrecks. As a friend, I could be her play pal and pitch in to help her do chores in half the time so we could dash out to a wild beach party. We could talk on the phone as phone friends and make silly comments about everyone but ourselves. This was fun to think about, but being in love, having a crush, an *infatuation*, was much more fun to wallow in. I spent hours sitting quietly in class while in my imagination I was holding her hand as I drove my customized dune buggy through the surf toward a setting sun. I dreamed of exchanging gifts each year on the anniversary of the first day we saw each other—I'd give her a pair of lovebirds in a golden cage in the shape of the Cape Hatteras Lighthouse, and she would give me a miniature portrait of herself painted inside the illuminated dial of a diver's watch.

I would look up into her eyes and boldly say, "I love you now, and *forever*."

She would stare down into my eyes and say, "I love you more."

"No," I would reply, and kiss the top of her extended hand. "I love *you* more."

"*Impossible*," she would whisper, swooning slightly. "I'm *crazy* about you."

I was back to wishing I were something I was not. I just couldn't help myself, and this kind of mindless fantasy conversation occupied my brain for most of the day. Still, a small part of me kept whispering in my ear, "Get a grip on yourself! You are in fourth grade. Grow up! Be a man!" Even though I knew my fantasy life was a complete waste of time, it was too blissful to resist.

As I sat in class I had to keep an eye on myself so she wouldn't catch me staring vacantly at her with honey-glazed eyes. Instead, I was sneaky. I dreamed my hazy love dreams while pretending to be interested in what she was saying. I tried to sit up straight at my desk and look as solid as a fifth president on Mount Rushmore. Had she ever given us a pop quiz, I wouldn't even have known what subject to fear. Half the time I didn't even realize I was in school, I was so wrapped up in the fantasy of her accepting my marriage proposal, which was simultaneously broadcast over the school intercom.

One afternoon while I stared out at her as if looking into the eyes of a hypnotist, I suddenly realized she had been standing in front of the entire class with her hands on her hips and a look on her face that meant she was cooking up something extra special for us to do. There were eighteen of us and slowly, one by one, boys and girls, we looked up from our work, or daydreaming, and realized she had a powerful thought she needed to share. So we waited. And waited. And waited, until the suspense was killing us. Our faces stretched toward her like flowers reaching for the sun. There was so much torque in the anticipation that it was nearly impossible to sit still in our chairs and we nearly popped out of them like old seat springs busting loose.

Finally, she raised her left pointer finger in the air and spoke with precise enunciation. "The great thinkers of the world have always claimed it is better to know one thing really well than to know a little about a lot of things," she declared. "Do you know what I mean?"

I raised my hand and started talking at the same time. "My mom always says it is better to buy one good thing than a lot of cheap junk."

"My point exactly!" she said. "A lot of junk is still junk. And a lot of bits and pieces of knowledge just makes you scatterbrained. So, I've come up with an as-

signment that you can really sink your teeth into—
something you can thoroughly immerse yourself in. I
want each of you to go home tonight and check your
bookshelves or go to the library or a bookstore and
think about what your favorite book is, then bring it in.
But choose carefully, because what we are going to do is
copy it word for word into our journals. This way, from
writing it down it will be as if *you* created it—each
word—each sentence—each thought—the style of the
writing—the voice—the range—the punctuation—you
will understand everything about how it was written.
And in the end, your favorite book will be etched into
your brain forever and you will know it so well you will
be able to recite it by heart to your children and grand-
children."

I don't know what the other kids thought, but I imagined she looked down at us like Cleopatra ordering her
loyal scribes to copy books onto papyrus for all of
mankind. She was incredible.

"Then, once we have all finished our books, we will
dress up as the main characters and parade through the
school, leading all the other kids into the auditorium for
a Reading Roundup. Then each of you will corral a
group of students and recite a passage, and in doing so
you will become the *living, breathing* book."

That part sounded a little scary because I wasn't good
at memorizing *anything* word for word. I knew kids who

could recite Lincoln's Gettysburg Address by heart, or Longfellow's *Hiawatha*. I was much better at just making something up than remembering what someone else had made up. My mind was always wandering just a little too much. But because Miss Noelle said it was a good project, I believed her and would try my best. Perhaps, I thought, I could just try to remember some funny poems from a joke book. I had memorized one already: *Billy built a guillotine, Tried it on his sister Jean, Said mother when she brought the mop, These messy games have got to stop.*

At the end of the day I wanted to go to the school library and check out a great book, but I couldn't. A few weeks before, I had left *Charlotte's Web* on a table in the cafeteria and it had disappeared. I figured someone would turn it in, but they hadn't. I thought of asking Mrs. Nivlash to make an announcement over the intercom, but I didn't want anyone to know I had been reading a book that Miss Noelle might think was below my reading level. Even though I loved Fern and Wilbur and Charlotte and her babies, I guessed I had outgrown the book. After all, now that I was becoming a man I needed more challenging reading, something more manly and *romantic*.

Since I hadn't saved up enough allowance to pay for *Charlotte's Web*, I had lost my library privilege. And at home I didn't have a shelf full of favorite books. We didn't even have bookshelves. But down the road we had a volunteer lending library. It was in a little pink beach shack between Midgett's grocery store and the mini–post office. The library wasn't staffed and was based on the honor system, which meant that if you took a book, you had to leave a book. I needed a book to donate, so I began to look around the house for one that nobody would miss. In our living room I spotted a rain-swollen copy of *Kon-Tiki* tilted up against the side of the window frame. Dad said it was about a boat that might disappear under the waves. I thought I'd help it disappear a little sooner.

I walked down to the lending library. A big sign on the door bluntly read: THERE IS NOTHING WORSE THAN A THIEF. It made me nervous because I had stolen things before, things I needed, like my sister's pen, or one of Pete's shoelaces, or the book I had in my hand. I opened the door and stepped inside. It smelled like seaweed. I waved my arm in front of my face to wipe away a spider's web, then squatted down to look over the selection. There were mysteries, histories, war sagas, self-help books, and romances. There were no children's books. But that didn't matter, because once I saw the romances I knew I had hit pay dirt. I grabbed one and read a few flowery sentences.

Her loveliness was infectious, for when she entered the ballroom the music stopped as if the conductor's hand were paralyzed, and heads spun in awe as quivering jaws dropped and knees bent. She was a vision of beauty, a vision as powerful as any seen by the ancients on the Acropolis or at Thebes or Troy. She was a gossamer goddess. An Athena, a Cleopatra, a Helen rolled into one. Grown men froze at the sight of her and women of typical beauty either fled the room or remained to serve her. And yet, she did not wish for obedience, but for equality, justice, and faith, and she was searching for a soul mate—a man of true compassion—a man of hope in a hopeless world.

It was the best writing I had ever read. I was sure of it. With each word I imagined Miss Noelle as the great beauty ruling the world with unwavering wisdom and grace. And I could be the compassionate *soul mate*, the man of *hope* she was searching for *in a hopeless world* to share her noble life of truth and justice. I squeezed the swollen *Kon-Tiki* into the empty slot on the shelf. I went straight home and began to copy the romance novel into my notebook. I figured if I got a head start on the copying, Miss Noelle would read mine first and *live* and *breathe* the book that defined me.

The next day we turned in our book choices. Miss Noelle stacked them on her desk and began to sort through the titles while we did some math problems. Every other moment I glanced up at her desk, because I had also turned in my journal and I wanted to catch her eye the moment she read the passage I had copied, which was the moment the great beauty met her great soul mate.

Finally she did look up at me. Her brow was furrowed. "Jack," she said, and I could tell by the way she paused she was carefully choosing her words, "may I speak with you?"

My heart beat wildly. I stood and walked to her desk with stiff dignity as if I were being called to receive the Pulitzer prize for my work on the subject of *hope*.

"Do you realize," she asked, "that you have to dress up as the main character in your book for the Reading Roundup?"

"Yes," I said, imagining myself more or less as a dashing prince.

"Then you must understand that the main character in the book is a woman and you would have to wear an eighteenth-century ball gown with beeswax makeup and jewelry."

I snapped out of it. "Oh no," I said, and suddenly had a vision of myself dressed up like Cinderella at the ball. The vision was all wrong.

"You might rethink this book choice," she said gently. "In fact, you might think about choosing a more traditional children's book. Something like *My Name Is Aram*, or *Johnny Tremain*. You know," she said, "a young man's book, like *Onion John*."

"I-I didn't think I'd have to dress like a girl," I stammered, blushing wildly. My face felt like a sputtering neon sign. "I was confused over the assignment," I said, trying to recover. "I'll get another book. A better book."

She smiled up at me. "That's a good idea," she agreed.

At the end of the day I strolled down to the school library to beg for permission to check out a book. But the librarian was unmoved. "No check in," she said, while pointing to the sign on her desk, "no check out!" It was her motto. "Now, if you pay for the book you lost, then you can choose any book you wish—except for the lost copy of *Charlotte's Web*."

"Can I trade you this book for another?" I asked, holding out the romance novel. She looked down at it as if it were a putrid thing I found crawling under a rock.

"No," she said, and curled up her lip.

"Could you make an exception?" I pleaded. "I'm a good kid. I—"

She cut me off. "Rules are rules," she recited. "Without them you have chaos, and I hate *chaos*."

"So do I," I said. "I love order."

"Then you better line up six hundred and ninety-five pennies in a row," she said.

She was right. "Okay," I said. "I'll do what I can."

When I returned home I picked up the newspaper.

There was a section under the heading UNCLAIMED
MONEY. Below it, in very small print, were listed the
names of people who were owed money by the state
but, for some reason I couldn't figure, had mysteriously
fallen out of touch with what was rightfully theirs. I began to search for my name. Maybe they owed me cash I
didn't know about.

"What are you doing reading the unclaimed money
section?" Betsy asked, looking over my shoulder.

"Digging for gold," I said. "I lost *Charlotte's Web* and
now I need to pay for it."

"That's what you get for reading that *baby* book. It's
turned your brain to mush."

"Not so," I said.

"You'd be better off looking for your name in the *Unclaimed Brains* section," she said. "There is only one way
to make money—*work* for it."

"Can kids apply for welfare?" I asked her.

"Of course not," she snapped at me. "Kids are the
cause of welfare!"

"Sorry I asked," I said, and slinked away.

When Dad came home, I asked him if I could borrow
a few dollars to buy a book for class. "Go to the library,"
he said.

"I can't," I said, hanging my head. "I lost a book."

"Then show some *ambition*," Dad replied. "Get a job

and pay for it. How old are you?" he asked suddenly, as if I were a stranger.

"Nine," I answered, knowing what he was going to say. He'd been saying it for years.

"By the time I was nine I was making my own money," he said proudly. "I wasn't a drain on my parents. My first job was as a delivery boy for a hardware store. I'd run the whole way from the store to the customer with a fifty-pound bag of cement on my back. And if it was a big order I'd run while pulling a wagon."

"Okay," I said. "But I thought there were laws against kids working."

"Nonsense," Dad replied. "Those laws were made by a bunch of government slackers who wanted to keep all the fun kid jobs to themselves." He swatted me across my rear with his sailor cap and pointed toward the front door. "Now, *hit-the-road-Jack-and-don't-come-back* until you have a job."

I walked across the street to the gas station. A guy in a blue jumpsuit with his name, *Kenny*, over a pocket filled with pens and tire-pressure gauges was sitting at his desk reading a muscle-car magazine. I thought I'd look sharp in a gas-station outfit. I could imagine gassing up Miss Noelle's car and having her think I looked ruggedly handsome in a jumpsuit with *Jack* embroidered over the pocket.

I coughed and Kenny glanced over at me then spit tobacco juice toward an empty grease can in the far corner. I didn't think Miss Noelle would like that habit.

"Excuse me," I said. "I'm looking for a job."

He looked me up and down as if I were made of scrap metal he was thinking of selling by the pound. "How old are you?" he asked.

"Fourteen," I said, lying.

"You aren't tall enough yet to ride a roller coaster," he said derisively. "If you're fourteen, I'm a hundred and fifty. I'll tell you one thing, kid, it's not a good policy to start off with a lie when you're trying to get a job where money changes hands."

"I'll just change tires," I said. "Or oil."

"This is a man's job," he said. "If I were you I'd just get a job washing cars, or pet sitting or mowing lawns or something. That's how I got started. You know, with *kid* jobs."

"But kid jobs just get kid pay," I said.

"Well, people don't want to pay a lot for piddling stuff," he said. "Go down to Midgett's grocery store and check out the bulletin board," he suggested. "That's where the locals post notices for little odds and ends of jobs. You have to start someplace."

He was right. "Thanks," I said. As I turned to go he spit toward the same can.

I went down to the grocery store and read the want ads. There was a listing for a "dog sitter." It wasn't far away and I walked over to the house. A sign on the door read, DOG IN. I flipped it over. It read, DOG OUT. I wasn't sure what that meant so I just rang the doorbell. A man with a handlebar mustache and a tattoo on his shoulder that read CAVE CANEM opened the door.

I puffed out my chest. "I'm here for the dog-sitting job," I explained.

"Come on in," he said.

I went inside. I didn't see the dog, but the floor looked like a battlefield of chewed-up dog toys. Gnawed bits and pieces were everywhere. He pointed to a chair. The legs were chewed down to matchsticks, and the seat was a thick mat of stiff fur. "Sit!" he ordered and snapped his fingers. I did.

He pulled a photo album off the shelf and flipped it open. "Okay," he said. "What I'm about to show you is for your own good. I just want you to know that when it comes to pets and pet sitters, I've had some lousy experiences. So I'm pretty careful about who I hire." He opened the album and showed me a photo of a big snake wrapped around his neck. "My beautiful python," he said wistfully. "This was when he was alive." Then he pointed to another photo. The snake looked sunburned. "The sitter," he growled, "thought the snake was cold and warmed him up in the oven."

"I'm sorry. Deeply grieved," I said, in my hushed funeral-parlor voice.

"And this one," he said, flipping the page. "My pot-bellied pig, Wilbur. Now, who would let a pig chew on an electrical cord?"

"I wouldn't," I said. "Only an idiot would." I was trying my best to sound indignant with the person who had done something so careless. Especially to a pig named Wilbur.

"Darn tootin'," he said. "Only a moron or a sadist would be so cruel."

"I'm not cruel," I said. "Honest."

He turned the page and I caught a glimpse of something that looked like a ferret strung up on a curtain cord. Or maybe it was a skunk.

"Could we not look at any more pictures?" I asked, feeling queasy, and guilty. The dead pets reminded me of a very bad moment in my life. I was mowing the lawn back in Pennsylvania when I accidentally ran over my uncle Bill's pet bunny. I'll never forget that moment when the mower bucked and something thumped around the blade housing and suddenly the bunny was blasted out in shreds across the grass. In my defense, it's important to point out that the grass was really high and that in honor of Saint Patrick's Day Uncle Bill had spray-painted the rabbit green.

"What's the matter?" the guy asked. "The photos get to you?"

"Yes," I said. Just then I heard a dog scratching on

the other side of a hallway door. It sounded like some-one who had suddenly awakened inside a coffin and was now desperately trying to get out.

"You better get going," he advised. "He's pretty ac-tive. Once I let him outside to do his business, I have to flip the sign to DOG OUT and let out a blast on my air horn so the neighbors know to call their kids in."

I trotted for the door.

"Do you want the job?" he asked.

"No," I said, and broke into a full sprint. As I ran down the sidewalk, I didn't think it would look very *romantic* if Miss Noelle saw me running from a dog I was supposed to walk. But I didn't care. Saving my skin was more im-portant than saving my reputation as a manly man.

That night I made up my own book. I titled it *Beware of the Dog* and it was all about a dog named Jack that was madly in love with its owner, who happened to be a beautiful fourth-grade teacher with blond hair. One day she was attacked by a student who went mad from star-ing at her radiant beauty and the dog saved her. From then on, the dog was always at her side and she fed him from her own plate and let him sleep at the foot of her bed on a yellow pillow with the name "Jack" embroi-dered in thread made from her own hair.

When I turned in my composition book the next day Miss Noelle held me after class.

"May I see the book you copied this from?" she asked, with her hand extended.

"It's my book," I said proudly as my eyes twinkled. "I wrote it myself."

She paused. "Jack, has that *infatuation* returned?"

I lowered my head. "Yes, Miss Noelle," I replied. "I can't help it."

"You have got to get over it," she demanded. "I can't have you sitting in the front row dreaming over me like some love-starved puppy dreaming about a bone. As you get older you are supposed to get *more* mature, not *less* mature. That's why I want you to read some books with *mature* young men in them."

"But I admire you . . ."

"Oh, stop it," she said impatiently, and waved her hand in front of my face. "Move on. You're a great kid. Now go pick on someone your own age. There are a lot of nice girls in class you can befriend."

"There's no one like you," I said, my voice melting away.

"You need a hobby," she suggested. "Do you have a pet?"

"No," I replied. "Just a younger brother."

"That doesn't count," she said. "You need something to take care of. Something you can smother with affection—and I don't mean a stuffed animal."

There was only one thing I wanted to smother with affection. I gave Miss Noelle my smitten look, with my head tilted to one side, and my eyelids half closed. I breathed deeply through my mouth.

"Go home," she ordered. "Before I give you extra homework."

That snapped me out of it.

I went home and felt totally defeated. Nothing was working out for me. I went out to the swamp and sat on a wet rock. Each time a mosquito landed on my arm, I smacked it as hard as I could. "You can't fall in love with your teacher," I said to myself. *Smack!* "You just have to do exactly what she tells you to do." *Smack!* "Grow up, get a *mature-boy* book and become the character." *Smack!* But what book?

And then a living book came waddling by. A mother duck was crossing the road with a long line of ducklings behind her. "Look," I said to no one. "It's Jack, Kack, Lack, Mack, Nack, Ouack, Pack, and Quack from *Make Way for Ducklings*." I remembered all their names because it wasn't too long ago that I had been reading that book a lot. I really loved it. Now I never touched it because I thought it was a baby book.

I looked back at the ducks as if they had the answer when I noticed there was something wrong with the last little duck. Quack kept flapping his wings and trying to catch up, but he'd just fall forward onto his beak, then flap his wings until he got upright, take a few more steps, and land on his beak again.

"Ouch," I said after he had fallen face first about ten times in a row, "that must hurt." I went over to him to see what was wrong, and when I looked at him close up I saw that his feet were on backward. The tips of his webbed feet were facing his tail, and his heels were facing his chin. He toppled forward again and just lay there, defeated. I waited for his mom to turn around and help him out but she kept walking and his brothers and sisters followed her, so I picked him up. He was just like me—defeated. I might have been able to accept it in myself, but I couldn't let it happen to a baby duck. I took him into my room and got a box and some dried-up sea grass to make a soft bed. I gave him bits of bread and he ate. Quack was cute, but I just couldn't take my eyes off the backward feet.

That night at the dinner table Dad asked, "Has anyone seen my copy of *Kon-Tiki*? I have ten pages left and want to know if that boat sank or reached land."

I knew I had to change the subject. "You won't believe what I found," I announced to Betsy. "A freak of nature."

"That was just you looking into a mirror," she said.

"No," I said. "I found a duck with backward feet."

"I don't believe you," she said flatly.

Everyone else looked suspicious. I jumped up and retrieved Quack from my room.

"But what can we do to help him?" I asked. I set him on the table and he toppled forward, beak first into the butter dish. "His own mother left him behind."

Mom picked him up and began to wipe his beak with her napkin.

"He's the weak link," said Betsy. "He has to be left behind to die. This is how each species rids itself of defects."

"Then why'd we keep you?" I shot back.

"So I could grow up and crush you," she replied.

"Well, maybe backward feet are not a defect," I said. "Maybe they are the beginning of something new and good. Maybe with his feet on backward he can swim faster in reverse and avoid trouble. Not everything strange is a problem. Look at flounders. They have eyes on one side of their head, which I think is clever, not ugly and weird. I wish we had eyes in the palms of our hands so we could stick them out and see around corners and in cracks and up over the tops of things. People might evolve in ways we don't even know yet. Maybe backward feet on a duck isn't a defect, it's *evolution*."

"Well, you've evolved into an idiot!" Betsy declared. She stood up and marched toward her room.

"Let's take him to the vet," Mom suggested. "Maybe she can do something." She set him on the table and he fell forward again.

"Yeah," Dad said, flicking cigarette ashes onto his dinner plate. "She'll be eating duck for supper. Betsy's right. You should put the duck out in the wild, and if it survives with backward feet, then fine. But if not, well, that's nature's way of keeping the species pure."

"But we can help," Mom said, petting him. "We don't let children die if they are born with a problem. We save them. We are a species that has learned to right some of the wrongs that are found in nature. We should take the duck to a vet."

"I'm saying," Dad said, "that if nature wanted that duck to live, it would have given him forward-facing feet."

"I guess," I said quietly. But something in me really felt for that little duck. Somehow I felt my crush on Miss Noelle was as backward as the duck's feet. We were both all turned around. I wanted to ask Mom what kind of doctor could give me a cure, but I didn't want to bring up the subject because I knew everyone would make fun of me.

The next day I didn't turn in anything to Miss Noelle. "I'm working on finding just the right book," I mumbled when she asked about my choice. I didn't look up at her or else I would start daydreaming again. I was like a person on a diet who didn't dare even glance at the refrigerator.

After school I carried Quack to the vet's office. I had always wanted to go inside because her building was shaped like Noah's Ark, with the heads of painted plywood animals looking out fake ark windows.

I was in luck. The vet had just finished with her last patient and took us right away.

"I've never seen anything like this before," she said. "Poor duck probably had its feet twisted around backward inside the egg and they didn't spring back around."

"My sister said it should die," I said.

"Well," she replied, "I feel differently. Once something is alive, it is our job to help it in life."

"That's what my mom thought," I said.

"You know," she said, "whenever I see an animal that people give up on I always remember Wilbur in *Charlotte's Web*. If it wasn't for Fern, he would have been sausage instead of being 'radiant.' "

I gave her a knowing glance because that was one of my favorite books and hers, too. "What can we do?" I asked.

"I think I can break the legs and twist them back around," she said. "I'll wrap them until they heal. It sounds awful but I think it will work."

"How much will that cost?"

"A good bit," she said.

"Can I work it off?"

"Sure," she replied. "We can do a barter deal."

"One more thing," I asked. "Do you happen to have a copy of *Charlotte's Web* I can borrow?"

"Yeah," she said pointing toward the door. "There are about a half-dozen of them in my waiting room. That book changed my life. That's why I became a vet. I was like Fern. I couldn't stand to see Wilbur killed."

"I've always felt a little like Wilbur," I confessed.

"We all do," she replied. "Now let me get working on this duck. And come back tomorrow and we'll figure out how you can help me around here."

"Thanks," I said, looking up at her with a funny feeling inside. Suddenly she seemed to be the most interesting and wonderful and compassionate person I had ever met. "And I'll work hard, too," I added.

On the way out the door I grabbed a copy of *Charlotte's Web*. That night I started copying the book. And when I got tired of copying, I flopped across my bed and read. Even though I had read it before, it was still so good I forgot all about my crush on Miss Noelle. Suddenly I realized I didn't need *older, more mature* books. Thinking that *Charlotte's Web* was too young wasn't the point. Discarding a favorite book was like throwing away the duck. That wasn't evolution. We could save the duck and I could save all the books I had ever read that meant something wonderful to me.

And when I finally finished the book and came up for air, I knew there was nothing I loved more than Charlotte and her children and Fern and Wilbur. Nothing. I had loved them the first time I read about them, and I'd love them forever—and now I just had to figure out which main character I'd dress as for the Reading Roundup.

Julian came to the door with a piece of chocolate money wrapped in gold foil. He held it out for Pete to see, but he wouldn't let Pete touch it. "It's real gold," Julian said. "And I have to sell it. Need the money to buy my Mom a birthday gift."

"Wow!" Pete said. "How much is it worth?"

That's when I stepped forward. "It's bogus," I said. "Worth about as much as a Hersey Kiss."

"It's not bogus!" Julian shouted back. "It's genuine gold and it's worth thousands of dollars."

I laughed out loud.

"Pete," Julian said, "I'll sell it to you for only ten dollars."

Pete looked up at me with his eyes all bugged out. "Ten bucks," he said like he was in a trance. "I have ten bucks."

"Best deal you'll ever make," Julian said quickly and elbowed me out of the way. He didn't want me to talk sense to Pete and ruin his scam, but I couldn't let hi~ ~~~

The Genius Test

"...trick," I sa~ ~~~ ~ the coin out of his hand.

"You give that back!" he shouted.

I held it away from him and tried to peel off the foil but Pete grabbed one of my arms and Julian grabbed the other. All I could do was bend forward and pop the coin into my mouth.

"He ate it!" Pete yelled. "Don't let him swallow."

Julian let go of my arm and grabbed me by the throat.

"I'm choking," I said.

"Spit it out," Julian said with his hands shaking my neck.

"Yeah, spit it out," Pete said.

To save myself I began to chew up the coin. I sucked out all the chocolate and crunched the foil into a little ball. I spit it out and it hit the floor and stuck there in a circle of brown spit. "There's your gold," I said.

Both Julian and Pete looked stumped, then Julian picked it up and his face brightened. "Hey Pete," he said suddenly. "How would you like to buy a genuine gold nugget?"

I'm a genius," Pete said. "Watch this." He stuck the TV remote out the window and pressed the button. I could hear Julian's TV suddenly change channels from a Dick Clark Music Special to a *Combat!* rerun.

All the Seabee families had just received the TVs. Dad and the other recruits had been complaining that they didn't make enough money to buy TVs, so the Navy surprised them with a bonus. A truck pulled up from Sears and each family received a Zenith TV with a remote control. It took Pete only a day to figure out how to drive Julian's dad crazy.

"Dang it," I heard his dad holler after Pete had changed his channel. "This remote's defective." Then I heard Dick Clark come on again. "There. That's more like it."

"Turn it up, Dad!" Julian hollered. I peeked out the window. Julian was hopping up and down on his couch playing air guitar. He spun around and spastically strummed on his belly as if he were on fire and was trying to put himself out.

Pete carefully aimed our remote at their window as if he were a sniper and in an instant turned their TV to a Tom and Jerry cartoon. We ducked.

"Dang it!" his dad yelled again. "What good's a remote if it has a mind of its own?" He must have thrown it because I could hear it hit the wall and clatter across the floor.

"You broke it!" Julian shouted mournfully.

"No, I didn't," he replied. "The cover just got knocked loose."

I started laughing. "That is *so* cool," I whispered to Pete.

"I'm a genius," he said matter-of-factly, and tapped himself on the head with the remote.

"No," I disagreed, "you are just sneaky. You are not a genius. There's a difference."

"You are dead wrong," he replied. "I've been thinking a lot lately and I now realize I'm a genius. I've been coming up with all kinds of genius ideas without even trying to think. Like, if you read a book backward the main characters never die. If you sleep all day and stay up all night you'll never need sunglasses. Thoughts just pop into my head. They even make a *popping* sound, like popcorn."

"More like the sound of a lightbulb blowing," I said.

Just then there was a knock at the door. It was Julian.

"Here comes trouble," I whispered. "I bet he's come to tell us his dad is going to beat us to a pulp if we don't stop changing the channels."

"I'll hide the remote," Pete said, and headed for the kitchen. "He won't know it was us if we can't find the remote."

"Sure, Einstein, that's a genius plan," I said sarcastically.

Julian pounded harder. "Hey, guys," he hollered. "I'm more than smart-smart-smart enough to know you are in there."

"We're here," I confirmed after Pete tossed the remote into the freezer. I walked toward the door. "What's up?"

"I just came to let you know that I'm a genius. I took a Gifted and Talented test at school and they said I'm so smart they might take me out of third grade and put me into fifth—then I'd be more advanced than you."

The genius virus was spreading faster than measles.

"They said I'm off the charts!" Julian bragged. "Charts! Charts! Charts!"

"They probably mean you are sailing in *uncharted water*," I suggested.

"No! *Off the charts!*" he repeated clearly. "Like, so smart they don't even have a category for me."

"Did you cheat?" I asked, squinting hard at him.

"Didn't have to cheat-cheat-cheat," he said, grinning. "So smart I don't need to."

"Well, I'm a genius, too," Pete announced, returning from the kitchen.

Julian's face dropped. It was obvious that he wanted to be the only genius in our Seabee trailer park. "What's your proof?" he asked, challenging Pete.

"Can't tell you," Pete replied. "It's a secret."

"Well, you need proof," Julian insisted, "or I won't believe you."

"You'll have to take my word for it," Pete said, and shrugged.

"Forget it," Julian replied, getting all huffy. "You're lying. You're just jealous of me because I'm smarter than you-you-you are."

"Don't be a jerk," Pete said.

"Don't be a jughead!" Julian shot back.

Suddenly Pete leaped on him and they fell over backward out the door and began to roll across the patchy front yard. "Say I'm a genius," Pete grunted. He was smaller than Julian but had surprised him and now had Julian's face down in the sand.

"You're a moron-moron-moron," Julian sputtered, and rolled back and forth, trying to shake Pete off.

"Say I'm smarter than you are," Pete ordered.

"I'm smarter than *you* are," Julian mimicked.

Pete became furious. He leaned forward and bit Julian on the top of his head.

"Stop it," I hollered, and ran at them. I grabbed Pete and pulled him away, and as I did so I noticed there was a hank of Julian's hair stuck between Pete's teeth. While Julian wiped the sand from his eyes, I quickly shot my hand out and snatched the hair from Pete's mouth. If Julian saw that, he'd go bonkers.

"Now, I want you two to apologize to each other," I demanded.

"No-no-no way," Julian replied. "A genius doesn't have to apologize to a Neanderthal."

Pete raised his fist.

I stepped between them. "Okay," I said. "I've had it with this fighting. As far as I'm concerned you are both mini minds. But to settle your argument, tomorrow I'm going to announce the rules of a Genius Test, and whoever wins gets to be the Seabee genius. But I set the rules and I'm the judge. Do you both agree?"

"Let's get it on," Julian said, squinting evilly.

"You mean, get on your dunce cap," Pete said, swaggering.

Julian stuck his nose in the air and turned away. As he walked home gently rubbing the sore spot on his scalp I whispered to Pete, "Why did you bite his head?"

"That's where his brain is," Pete replied. "It was like going for his throat."

"You're weird," I said.

"All geniuses are misunderstood," he replied proudly, and drifted off as if he were a cloud in the shape of himself.

By the next afternoon I had come up with a test. The three of us gathered in front of school, where I explained it. "There will be four categories—memory, inventions, sneakiness, and literature."

"Does that mean I can write a song-song-song for the literature category?" Julian asked.

"Sure," I said. "But no help from your dad."

"Can I write a poem?" Pete asked.

"You can write a novel," I said. "But first we have to work on the first category—memory. Now listen. The true sign of a genius is found in one universal factor," I announced, "a photographic memory."

"I have a great memory," Julian declared, tapping himself on the side of his head. "I'm a living jukebox. I know every song lyric ever recorded."

"I've never forgotten anything," Pete bragged. "I even remember the moment I was born."

"Well, let's do a scientific test to determine if either of you has a genius memory," I said. "Here's how it's going to work. Today, when we walk home from school I want you to memorize every step of the way—every shell you step on, every curb, every pile of sand, every smell, every direction we turn—*everything*. And then tomorrow I'll blindfold you both and you'll have to walk home alone and if you have a photographic memory you'll have no problem. You'll make it home safe and sound."

"Okay," Pete said, snapping his fingers. "Sounds easy."

Julian smirked. "I can do that blindfolded *and* walking backward."

"Whatever," I said. "Now, let's walk home and along the way remember *everything*."

They walked home like dogs that had to stop and pee on every bush, every tree, every curb. They sniffed. They counted steps. They licked their fingers and held them up in the wind to mark its direction. It took us forever.

The next day after school I tied a red bandanna around Pete's eyes and one around Julian's. I stood them both on the exact spot in front of the flagpole where we had started the day before. "Ready?" I asked.

"Yes-yes-yes," Julian said.

"Ditto," Pete replied.

"Go!"

They started walking tentatively, with their hands held forward, squeezing at the air like blind lobsters. I watched as they slowly meandered across the school's front yard and turned right on the sidewalk. They zigzagged around and past each other like two sailboats tacking back and forth. "No cheating," I yelled out, tagging behind.

"Shut up," Julian yelled back. "I'm concentrating!"

"Yeah," Pete yelled. "All geniuses need mental solitude."

"You'll get plenty of that in a nut ward," I shouted back.

Just then Miss Noelle pulled up beside me. "Hi," she said, "need a ride home?"

Instantly I forgot all about Julian and Pete. "I'd *love* a ride home," I said, sounding like Alfalfa having a meltdown in front of Darla. I got in and we zoomed off.

"Who were those two boys?" she asked. "They had their eyes covered up."

"A couple of morons," I replied. "I hardly know them. By the way, do you know I'm a genius?"

She looked at me and smiled. "In that case, I think you need some challenging homework," she said thoughtfully. In a minute she gave me an assignment that combined bird migration and geography and geometry and the rotation of the earth and wind patterns and rainfall charts and insect growth ratios. I was completely mixed up. When she dropped me off in front of my trailer, I was relieved.

"See you tomorrow," I said with my head spinning.

She smiled slyly. "Good luck writing that ten-page paper," she hollered, and hit the gas.

Suddenly I was hot. I went inside, drank a glass of cold water, then stepped outside to see how the geniuses were progressing. In a minute I heard Pete wailing, then I saw him running for the house with the bandanna swinging loose in his hand. "Jaaaack!" he cried. "Jaaaaack! Help me."

I ran toward him. "What's wrong?" I asked. "What?"

"Look at my front tooth," he cried out, with a whistle.

I looked. Half of the left one was chipped off. "What happened?" I asked. "Did you two fight again?"

"No. I was doing everything just fine—just like a genius—when I walked into a parked car and hit the door handle with my teeth."

"Then you must have been off course," I said, already trying to deflect the blame.

"No!" he yelled angrily. "No! I was right on course, step by step, like a real genius. It's just that yesterday when I remembered my way home the car wasn't there and today it parked across my path."

"Oh," I said. "I hadn't considered that."

"Which is why you *aren't* a genius," he was quick to point out. "Or you would have figured something like this could have happened."

"Are you going to tell Mom and Dad about this?" I asked.

"Just depends," he said, "on how you score the test."

Before I could remind him that it was up to me to

play fair, I heard Julian crying as he hobbled toward us
without his bandanna.

"What happened to you?" I asked when he limped up
to us and miserably plopped down onto the sand.

"I stepped on a conch shell and twisted my ankle," he
explained. "It's no fair-fair-fair."

"Well, this test is a tie," I declared with great author-
ity. "You both removed your bandannas and are dis-
qualified."

"It was a stupid test," Pete said with a whistle.

"Tomorrow will be better," I promised. "We'll meet
right back here after school."

The next day we gathered out front for the inventions test.

"I want to go first," Julian insisted. "I have a good
one."

"Okay," Pete said. "Give it your best shot."

"Go put on your jeans and jean jacket," Julian instructed. "And I'll meet-meet-meet you out behind my
house."

Pete and I did.

"I've invented the perfect baby-sitting device to keep
a baby in one spot," Julian announced. "I call it the
Staple-Sitter, and I'm going to make millions on it."

He had Pete stand on an upside-down bucket with his
arms spread out against the wall like an angel. Then,

with a heavy-duty stapler, he stapled Pete's jeans to the wall with hundreds of staples. When Julian finished he kicked the can out from under Pete's feet. Pete didn't drop an inch. He didn't even sag a little.

"Lean forward and try-try-try to get out of it," Julian ordered.

Pete tried. He grunted and wiggled but was entirely fixed to the wall.

Julian tapped himself on the head with the stapler. "Genius," he declared. "I'm *so* off the charts."

Pete must have known it was a good one. He was pouting. Then in a sudden fit of poor sportsmanship, he yelled out, "He stole my idea!"

"No way," Julian protested. "I couldn't have stolen it from you because I stole it from my dad. He used to do this to me backstage when it was his night to watch me-me-me while he had a rock 'n' roll gig."

Pete frowned.

"Okay," I said. "Let's get Pete off of here." We stood on either side of him and began to pull on his jeans until the staples let go. Pete began to sag, and when he finally got off the wall we helped pull the staples out of his clothes.

"Now it's your turn," I said to Pete.

He didn't look very confident. "Okay," he sighed. "My invention is called the Tooth-Flute." He began to whistle out of his mouth and, by using his finger as a valve over the new gap in his front tooth, he began to play "Frère Jacques."

"That is so *bogus!*" Julian declared. "It's as if-if-if you are having a *psychotic* moment."

I could tell Pete knew he was beaten, so I didn't allow time for Julian to gloat. That was the best I could do.

"Julian is now in the lead, one to nothing," I declared. "But let's move on to the sneakiness category." I figured Pete would score well on this one.

"I'm not telling my idea," Pete said. "My genius sneaky idea is a secret."

"Then I'm not telling either," Julian said. "But it is a genius-level idea."

"Well, you both have to tell me," I insisted, throwing my hands up in the air. "Otherwise I won't be able to judge it."

"I won't tell unless he tells," Julian said, and began to laugh. "But believe me, it is beyond anything Wile E. Coyote could think of."

"I think you are lying," Pete said. "You just don't have a good idea."

"Then let's hear-hear-hear yours," Julian said.

"I can't tell you," Pete replied. "It's so top secret that it is *classified* by the government."

"Okay, boys," I said. "Okay. Let's just skip the third category."

"So who is the genius?" Julian asked.

"Yeah," said Pete. "Who?" He gave me a look like he expected me to rig the results in his favor.

"Let's move on to the literature category," I said a bit impatiently.

Pete frowned.

"I'll go first," Julian said. "Naturally, I made up a genius song. It will be the theme song for my TV show. Every week my show will open and show me doing genius things while my song plays in the background. Here goes: *I'm so smart, I'm off the charts . . . My brain's so huge there are no replacement parts . . . I solve problems all day long . . . I'm the world's answer man singing a song. La, la, la . . .*"

Pete fell down laughing. "What's the name for your show?" he asked. "*Looney Tunes?*"

"I am not-not-not amused," Julian said dryly, and stuck his nose into the air. "So, what is your genius bit of literature?"

Pete pulled himself together. "I have written a poem," he said, squaring his shoulders and loudly clearing his throat. "*Roses are red, Violets are blue, My IQ's so big, No hat will do.*"

"That's dumb," Julian said. "IQs don't wear hats."

"You're an idiot," Pete shot back. "And you will *always* be an idiot because there are no *replacement parts* for your pea-sized brain."

"Let's just fight-fight-fight," Julian said. "Winner is the genius. Loser is the moron!"

I jumped between them. "No more fighting," I said. "Fighting is for brain-dead boneheads."

"Then who is the winner?" Julian asked.

"Yeah?" said Pete.

"It's a tie," I said. "Pete's poem won the literature category."

"That's totally bogus!" Julian protested.

"Hey," I snapped back. "I don't want any lip from either of you. Not a word."

"So what do we-we-we do next?" Julian asked.

"I'll think of a tiebreaker tonight," I said, "and I'll announce it in the morning."

That night I worked on Miss Noelle's homework assignment and didn't make up the final test until we were all walking to school the next morning.

"Here is the final test," I announced. "As we all know, staying out of trouble at school is the sign of true genius. So, I want each of you to spend the whole day at school without ever going to class and without ever being sent to the principal's office. You will have to use all your genius skills to both avoid being absent while never being present."

"I don't get it," Julian said. "You want us to be-be-be invisible?"

"Invisible, but present at the same time," I replied.

"I think I get it," Pete said. "You just hang out in the hall around the front office and if anyone asks what you are doing, you just say you are waiting for the secretary to call your mom because you have head lice."

"Yeah," I said. "Something like that."

"It would be better," Julian said, "to just tell-tell-tell everyone you are a substitute custodian and push a broom around."

"Why don't you just hang out in the bathroom all day and if a teacher comes in tell them you have a contagious kidney infection," I suggested.

"I'm psyched for this test," Julian said, rubbing his hands together.

"Piece of cake," Pete said.

"One final thought," I added. "Remember, Einstein said, 'Imagination is more important than knowledge.' "

After we walked through the front door of the school they scattered.

During the day I received permission to go to the bathroom twelve times, but never spotted them. I sneaked out to the courtyard and climbed up into the replica of the Cape Hatteras Lighthouse. They were not there. And they were not hunkered down inside the model of the Wright brothers' first airplane. I volunteered to take a note from Miss Noelle to the front office and didn't see them there. They did not come out for morning recess, or lunch, or they were hiding behind the shelves in the library when I went there for more bird migration research. There was only a half-hour left in the day when suddenly the fire alarm went off.

"Okay," Miss Noelle directed. "You know what to do. Drop everything and follow me."

We did. All eighteen of us marched down the hall and joined the lines of other kids streaming out of classrooms. I stood on my tiptoes and searched for Pete and Julian. But I didn't see them. We all gathered on the back playground. There was a funeral and kids rushed the fence to get a good look. I kept moving through the crowd, looking for Julian and Pete. What if the school is on fire? I said to myself. What if there is a gas leak and it's going to blow up? What if a giant tidal wave is coming our way? I should tell someone, I thought. I turned and walked toward the open door.

"Jack Henry," Miss Noelle shouted. "Get over here with our class."

I trotted over to her. "What if someone is trapped in there?" I asked.

"It's a false alarm," she said. "Some pinhead pulled the switch in the cafeteria. The janitor told me. If it were a real fire, the heat would have set off the sprinkler sensor."

"Are you sure?" I asked.

"Yeah," she said.

Then it occurred to me that one of them might have

gotten hungry and this would be a way to sneak into the kitchen and get some food. But that seemed impossible. Pulling a fire alarm when there was no fire was the stupidest thing in the world. Neither of them was a genius, but they weren't that dumb either.

Soon the fire trucks came, and five minutes later they left. We were all herded back into the school and, still, I never saw Pete or Julian. It wasn't until I was leaving at the end of the day that I saw them drifting off, blending in with the other kids, bent over from the weight of their backpacks. I ran after them.

"Hey, wait!" I shouted. "I've been looking for you two everywhere. Where've you been?"

"You told us to hide," Pete said.

"Yeah," Julian said.

"But didn't you hear the fire alarm?" I asked.

They nodded.

"Did either of you pull it?"

"No," they said in unison. "That would be criminal."

"Then you're both morons. The school could have been in flames. A hurricane could have been heading toward us. A real genius would have realized it was smarter to be safe than to win some dumb contest. You both lose. The only thing you have won is the *idiot* contest."

"I'm no-no-no idiot," Julian said, grinning. "I hid in the crawl space under the auditorium stage all-all-all day and made up some new songs. Want to hear one?"

"Spare me," I said.

"And I squished myself into my locker all day," Pete said. "I felt like a candy bar inside a wrapper. I learned how to sleep standing up. I'm no idiot either."

But they were. They were idiots—mini minds—and that night it was confirmed.

I was watching a *Twilight Zone* rerun when, by itself, the channel changed. I knew who it had to be. "Hey, Pete," I called out. "Come in here and watch TV with me." He came in from the kitchen. Suddenly the channel changed again. Then again. "Oh my," I shouted toward the window at the top of my lungs. "What's going on?"

"What are you doing?" Pete asked.

"I'm encouraging a genius," I whispered. He looked puzzled.

"I love this TV show," I said loudly to Pete. Suddenly the channel changed.

"Are you doing this?" Pete asked.

"No," I said. "It's your *genius* friend across the swamp. The two of you are on the same *genius* level."

I walked over to the window. "Hey, genius!" I yelled. "Stop changing our channels."

He popped up from under his windowsill. "I'm a-a-a genius!" he yelled. "Watch this." He pointed the remote at our house and the TV changed again.

"Hey," Pete yelled back. "This was my top-secret sneaky genius idea."

"No, this is *my* sneaky genius idea."

"I'm the real genius," Pete claimed, waving the remote over his head.

"No-no-no way," Julian shot back. "I'm the true genius."

It takes one to know one, I thought, as Julian turned our TV on and off and flipped through the stations. Pete did the exact same thing to them. The battle of the remotes was going full blast and that's when I figured out what their special genius really was—driving us all insane.

After they had spent about twenty minutes changing each other's channels, I looked over at Pete. "Why don't you two start a *genius* club together," I said.

"That's a great idea," he replied. "But you can't join because you're not a genius."

"But I can join," Julian shouted. "Because I'm a genius!"

I got up and went into my bedroom. I was getting a headache. I needed a good book to read. "TV," I muttered, "it brings out the *genius* in everyone."

The Jr. Naval Cadets decided to take us on a field trip. "Now, no funny business," my Dad warned me after what had happened before with the raccoon problem. On Saturday they rented a Sea Bees bus and off we went to visit Walter Raleigh's "Lost Colony." He had landed in North Carolina in 1585 but couldn't make a go of it and he and a few survivors Returned to England in 1586. In 1587 another group returned but were wiped out without a clue. Nothing was ever found but a few wooden posts in the ground that were part of Fort Raleigh's walls. There was also a replica of his ship, the Elizabeth the II, and that was our true destination. The Jr. Naval Cadet leaders had wanted to take us to Annapolis, but couldn't raise the money. All the way down on the bus we sang, "ninety-nine bottles of beer on the wall," until we got to the last bottle and then began to sing pirate songs, and finished with, "Row, row, row your boat." When we got to the hotel we were treated like convicts. ~~~~ "~~~~ ~~~~ rooms had been espe ~~~~ The irons, and ~~~~ dryers were re ~~~~ V chan-nels that were ~~~~ ~~~~were four boys to a room and once in we had to stay in for the night. So we had a boiled egg snack out in the parking lot and then were marched into our rooms. To make sure nobody snuck out the leaders stuck a long strip of duck tape

over the door crack in the hallway and then one of them sat
guard duty all night. I knew it
was my Dad because of his snoring.
We had a door from our room into
the next room and we didn't destroy
anything, but we moved every
stick of furniture from one
room into the other. It was great
fun and the biggest stunt
I've ever done. We left before
all the rooms were inspected.
Ft. Raleigh was a bore compared
to the thrill of quietly moving
all that heavy furniture through
a narrow door.

The bathroom in our house trailer was very small. When you sat on the toilet your knees nearly touched the back of the door. The sink was the size of a salad bowl. My face just barely fit inside the frame on the wall mirror. Only half of Dad's face fit and he had to shift back and forth to shave both sides. But it was the only private room in the house—semiprivate, really, because anyone on the outside could hear what was happening on the inside. When Dad took a long shower after work and sang all the colorful verses of "Barnacle Bill the Sailor," Mom made us play out behind the swamp.

Even though I knew the bathroom was about as private as covering myself with a bedsheet in the middle of the living room, it was the place I retreated to when I needed to cry. I knew everyone could hear me sobbing away, but I just didn't want them to see my face. When I cried, my face got all screwed up like a washcloth being wrung out. I'd rather be seen naked and smiling than dressed and crying. It just seemed that crying in public was asking for trouble—especially with Betsy around. Whenever I was at my weakest, she became an even bigger bully than normal.

I was crying, not because of anything that had happened in my family, but for what had happened in trailer number two, where Mr. Hancock lived. He was divorced and had a son, Elliott, who lived with his mom on the mainland. From time to time Elliott came to visit. He was in a wheelchair and his dad always drove him around in the bed of his pickup truck. That's how Elliott liked it. His dad built a little ramp to wheel him up where Mr. Hancock could secure him in a special rack. After the ride he could wheel Elliot down. Elliott was very pale and thin and his arms always seemed to quiver for an awkward moment before he kind of jerked them into motion, like he first needed an electric shock to get himself going. The same with his speech. It was as if his lips were out of sync with his thoughts, and he could only talk one syllable at a time, as if the words had been snipped apart with scissors. He had always been in a chair and, from what we knew, wasn't doing very well. Word got around that there was some chance he was going to die and so his dad had me and Julian over to the house to be Elliott's friends for a day. We both understood we were supposed to be extra nice and, regardless of all my mom's warnings, we were. We had great fun playing Wiffle ball indoors and rubber-band warfare and game after game of ticktacktoe. That was Elliott's favorite game, and when he started first there was no beating him. It was the one thing he had going for himself, and he was proud of it. He knew he beat us fair and square, unlike when we played Wiffle ball and gave him as many strikes as he needed. Then after he hit the ball, one of us would drop it, while the other one would wheel him around the living room for an inside-the-park home run. He flopped around in his chair and laughed, but there was some understanding in his eyes that told me he knew we were faking. Or maybe he just always knew whatever fun he was having was temporary because soon it would *all* be over with.

Still, we all enjoyed the visit. It was fun being espe-cially nice and by the end of the day we really liked the kid. And when he said *goodbye* he whispered the word as though he didn't want to wake it up. That was the last time I saw him alive.

So earlier in the day, when Elliott's dad knocked on our door and stepped inside and quietly told me that Elliott had died, I was really struck by the news. I didn't know what to say. I just kept repeating, "I'm sorry. I'm so sorry. I'm so very sorry. I'm so very, very sorry." I couldn't stop myself from adding an extra *very* each time I expressed just how sorry I was. And I couldn't keep my mouth shut because I knew as soon as I stopped talking, I *would* be sorry and all the pain of it would hit me and I wanted to hold that pain off for as long as I could. So even after Mr. Hancock left, I kept saying, "I'm so very, very, very." With each *very* I took a step down the hall until, after twenty *very*s, I was in the bathroom with the door closed against my knees. I thought of Elliott and right away my chin quivered and my face twisted up and the tears ran hot down my cheeks and I cried so loud that my mom knocked on the door.

"Honey," she called gently, "are you all right?"

"Yes," I replied, sniffling. "I'm fine." And then I bit down on my lower lip to keep from crying, but soon enough my chin started quivering and then I was right back at it.

Between sobs I heard Mom say, "Just give him some time. He's sensitive. He'll be out in a minute."

"Well, I can't hold it any longer," Dad replied. "I think I'm going to have to go back to nature." In a minute I heard a beer pop open as he clomped down the hall and out the back door to pee in the bushes like he usually does when the bathroom is occupied.

Mom was wrong. I knew I could stay in the bathroom crying all night or until either she or Betsy would have to go and then I'd be flushed out of my hiding spot to cry in public. I couldn't bear the thought of Betsy making fun of me. So when I thought the coast was clear, I opened the bathroom door and dashed to my room. Pete wasn't there and I swung myself out the window and down onto the strip of dry ground next to the swamp. I wiped my face on my shirtsleeve and went over to Julian's window and peeked in. He was building a plastic warship from a kit. I didn't know if he knew about Elliott's dying because Julian's dad and Mr. Hancock had a falling-out at work over stolen tools and weren't talking.

"Let's take a walk," I said to Julian, and wiped my nose on my forearm.

"Can't," he replied. "I'm grounded for-for-for life."

"Why?"

"We were at my cousin's wedding. He was having it at his house. He's like nineteen and all my life he's been a jerk-jerk-jerk to me. So I climbed out a second-floor window and was just hiding out on top of the roof getting away from everyone when a crazy thing happened. The bakers were delivering the wedding cake, which looked-looked-looked something like a pirate ship with the bride and groom in the crow's nest. It was pretty cool. But like I said, I never liked him, so as they carried the cake across the yard I started singing, *Here comes the bride . . . one ton and wide! I'd rather kiss a pig-pig-pig in a wig . . . everyone hide!* Then I did my nut dance and lost my balance and rolled off the roof. I missed most of the cake but-but-but clipped off the mast and crow's nest and the bride and groom and when the bakers started yelling and everyone came out and saw cake and icing all over my shoes, they went ballistic and my cousin threatened to kill me, and my parents did, too."

"What happened next?" I asked.

"I started hollering that it was an accident and that I had fallen out a window and somersaulted off the roof and by coincidence the cake-cake-cake was passing by."

"Did they believe that?" I asked.

"Not really," he said. "But it's kept them from killing me, so they've just grounded me for life. I wrote a song about it," he said. "Do you-you-you want to hear it?"

"Love to," I said.

He stood up on his bed and struck a guitar-playing pose with one hand out on the imaginary neck of the guitar and the other scratching at his belly. "Okay," he said. "Imagine this played as loud and fast as humanly possible." Then he got a faraway look in his eyes and stared out over my head as if addressing the crowd at a rock concert. "Here's my new hit song that you all have been waiting for. It's dedicated to my cousin and it's called, 'I'd Do It Again!' "

Then he gritted his teeth and started strumming his air guitar and bouncing all over his bed. *I'd do it again!* he screamed. *"I'd jump on the cake. He's a jerk to me. And she's a-a-a fake!"* Then he went into an air-guitar frenzy and caromed all over his room and flipped over his ship model before landing back up on his bed for the second verse. *"I'd do it again!"* he wailed at the top of his lungs. *"I'd ruin their fun! I'd laugh at their wedding! Then run! Run! Run!"* He jumped off the bed again and started kicking holes in his door and rolling across the floor and punching the walls. The whole house rocked back and forth. "Somebody *help* me!" he yelled. "I'm *possessed!*"

"Julian!" his mother hollered, and whipped his door open. "You're already in enough trouble. If you trash your room you'll be sleeping outside. You hear me?" She pointed a very real frying pan at him.

His face dropped. "Yes, Mom," he replied. "I-I-I was only playing rock star."

"Well, try acting your age," she said. "Rock stars are *infantile!*"

"Okay," he said glumly.

"*And,*" she said, steaming up, "if you claim you're possessed one more time, I'll let the local priest knock the devil out of you, and believe me, they use more than a frying pan!"

"Yes, Mom-Mom-Mom," he said, and picked up a toppled chair.

Then she caught sight of me. "You!" she hollered with the frying pan held out like she had a tennis racket and was about to return a volley. I ducked down and began to slosh through the swamp on the way over to my house.

"You little coward!" she yelled again from the window. "You better run! I think you are a bad influence on my boy. You're giving him bad ideas. He was a good boy until you came along."

I didn't stop to argue with her. I thought Julian was a great kid. He was full of his own wild ideas and didn't need any of mine to get him worked up. But I didn't want to get my head flattened just to tell her so.

As soon as I reached for the front-door knob I heard Mom and Dad talking in the living room. I stopped to listen.

"He's a boy," Mom said. "For my own selfish reasons I'd love to see him stay a boy forever, but in the blink of an eye he's going to be bigger than both of us. And he can only grow into being a great man if we start young and raise a great boy."

"That's not true," said Dad. "I didn't start being a man until I turned thirty and look how I turned out."

"That's just what I'm talking about," Mom said sharply. "He needs guidance. Something wholesome to do, like Boy Scouts, or a sport."

"I don't have time for that stuff," Dad said. "The Navy works my tail off all day long."

"Well, you better make time, mister. You don't want

him turning out like that wild *problem* child across the swamp." I knew she was pointing toward Julian's house.

"Okay," Dad said. "I'll think of something."

"And don't just take him across the street to go fishing," she said. "Or rent a dune buggy and race around for your own kicks. You have to talk to him about things. Help him figure out the world. You can't just fish in the dark and *brood* all evening like you do. God, the last thing I want you to do is teach him how to brood."

I could hear Dad stand up and stomp across the room.

"Don't walk away from me when I'm being serious," she said. "We have to talk about this. Every time I want to talk, you want to walk. But if we don't talk about problems, we won't solve anything around here."

But Dad wasn't talking. He yawned loudly, like a lion. "I'm exhausted," he said, stomping in circles as if tramping down the tall grass and making a bed. "Time to call it a day."

The next night after dinner Dad looked over at me. "Hey, sport," he said. "Get my fishing rod and let's go over to the beach for a spell. It's time to spend a little time together, man to man."

I smiled. I knew what that was all about. "Great," I

said. I got his pole ready, put a few beers in the cooler, and grabbed a blanket. He carried his tackle box and a flashlight, and a hammer—just in case he caught something so big he had to give it a crack to calm it down.

"See you later," I called, waving to Mom.

But she didn't respond. She was glaring at Dad. "Remember what I told you," she said. *"Talk!"*

"Don't worry," Dad replied. "With my fishing luck, that's all I can do."

We crossed the road in front of the house and walked up over the dunes and down the beach a bit before getting set up. Right after Dad had cast out and we had settled down on the blanket, he began to talk.

"Don't listen to your mother," he said. "Brooding is good. She misunderstands what brooding means. Let me tell you. When a man is brooding, he is taking big troubles and working them down into little troubles. You know how in the movies they always show prisoners using sledgehammers to pound boulders into gravel?"

"Yeah," I said.

"Well, that's what I do in my mind." He tapped the side of his head. "When I'm quiet, I'm just grinding big worries down into a pile of dust and at the end of the evening I just blow them away and go to bed and sleep like a baby."

"So, why does Mom call that brooding?" I asked.

"Because your mom works her problems out differently," he said. "She likes to talk about everything. Talk, talk, talk. But a man needs his silence, and because she doesn't understand silence, she calls it brooding."

"I see," I said.

"Now, what's your problem?" he asked.

I took a deep breath and looked up into the night sky. Between two oval clouds, the stars looked like they were trapped in an hourglass. "I'm just sad about Elliott dying," I replied. "It's not fair. He was just a kid like the rest of us and he never did anything bad and now he's dead."

"Well, you just sit here silently and let the gears in your mind grind down all your troubles about that Elliott boy. Death is a tough subject, but I guarantee you that before long you'll feel a lot better."

So while Dad fished and remained silent—brooding, I guessed, about his own Navy problems—I thought about Elliott. I was relieved at first that it was dark out because I thought if I began to cry, Dad wouldn't see my face all screwed up. And with the wind blowing, maybe he wouldn't hear me whimper. But I didn't cry. Instead, the more I sat there the angrier I got. It seemed my head would explode. Life was unfair. The world was unfair. The universe was unfair. Why should Elliott die? It seemed so unjust when hundreds of people everywhere did awful things and got away with it and were never punished, but some poor kid in a wheelchair whose one joy in life was playing ticktacktoe was now dead. It really made me angry.

"Hey, Dad," I said, after my thoughts got the best of me.

"Yeah?"

"Maybe I'm not very good at brooding yet," I said. "I'm just getting madder and madder and I'm not grinding anything down to dust. What should I do next?"

"Hmm," he said. "Well, sometimes instead of solving anything from brooding, you just smolder. It's a bad form of brooding. You get stuck on a subject and you can't seem to get it out of your system no matter what."

"Then what do you do? Because I think I'm smoldering. I'm really mad about it. I thought I was going to be sad. But I'm more angry. And that's confused me. Because I thought my problem was going to get smaller but it just seems the more I brood, the bigger and worse it gets."

"Let me give you some advanced brooding lessons," he said. "First, if I'm smoldering over some work problem I take a walk along the beach. You know, just listen to the ocean waves crashing on the shore. Wave to the boaters. Breathe in the good sea air. Maybe you can let your mind drift along and think about what you like and don't like, who you are and who you are not, and what you want to become and what you don't want to become. Stuff like that."

"So, were you smoldering tonight?" I asked, standing up and getting ready to take a walk.

"No," he said calmly. "I was beyond smoldering. I was just thinking about sweet nothing."

"Nothing?" I asked, unconvinced.

"Nothing," he said firmly.

"How can you think of *nothing*?" I asked. "I'm always thinking. My eyes keep seeing, and I hear stuff. I *have* to think."

"It takes practice," he said. "Knowing how to be quiet, how to be still, how to think about nothing is one of the secrets to life. Thinking of *nothing* and brooding are related. First you brood until you grind your troubles down to *nothing*. Then you are totally happy. You are like that Buddha. You just sit and meditate all day over nothing and it's the best feeling in the world. If I had all the money I wanted, then I'd have no troubles. But I'm not rich in that way. So, when I'm thinking of *nothing*, it means nobody bothers me. Nobody can get into my head and bug me. Nobody. It's the poor man's way of being rich."

"I'm confused," I said.

"Well, why don't you just start off simple and try walking down the beach?" he said. "Try it. You'll catch on fast."

I started walking down the beach but I hadn't taken a few steps before I started getting angry all over again. Even thinking about Miss Noelle didn't distract me. I tried to think of us sailing on a gold-and-white yacht across a blue sea. We were smiling. Laughing. Not a trouble in the world. But then the image of us fizzled in my mind. I was *too* angry. Elliott should never have died. I turned around and marched back toward Dad. Before I bugged him again, I stood in the dark and watched him. Car headlights swept the beach and flashed across his face. He just sat there, looking out at the water, slowly sipping a beer and plucking on the fishing line, feeling for a bite. For a long time I watched his face. He was totally relaxed. Content. There was nothing on his mind he needed to say.

"How'd it go?" he asked when he saw me creeping up on him. He reeled in his line all the way until the silver spoon was hanging off the tip of the rod like a tongue full of hooks.

"I still have my work cut out for me," I said. "I can brood. I can smolder. But I can't seem to get to *nothing-ness*."

"Give it some time and practice," he said. "You'll get there."

I picked up the blanket and waved it overhead. The sand blew away from us. I could only wish my sadness and anger would follow.

The next day I went over to Julian's window and peeked in. He was sitting at a little side table with a plate of food. He was drinking a glass of milk. I guessed he was so grounded he had to eat in his room, like Max in *Where the Wild Things Are*.

"Hey," I said, "did you hear? Elliott died."

"I know," he replied. "I already made up a new song for my dad's band. What to hear it?"

"Sure," I said.

"It's not really a rock song and it's not really a folk song. It's just sort of a ballad. So picture me sitting on-stage, on a tall black stool with my acoustic guitar and a single spotlight on me."

"Okay," I said.

"*Elliott was nice,*" he sang softly, strumming his fake guitar as if he were petting a cat. "*Elliott was sweet. Life was mean to him, but he didn't dig defeat . . . He's circling the world, spinning like a ring, his soul set loose like a kite out of string.*"

"That's beautiful," I sighed, tearing up.

He took a bow.

I was clapping when his mother entered the room. "You again!" she shouted.

As I tried to duck out of sight, I saw her hand snatch Julian's glass of milk off his table and pitch it toward me.

The glass shattered against the wall.

"Get out of here!"

I turned and ran across the road, up and over the dunes, and began to walk along the shore. The sun was setting and the whitecaps looked pink, then purple, and as I circled home they were gray. The walking helped because when I thought about Julian's mom throwing milk at me I began to laugh. It seemed so silly, like a cartoon playing over and over until it faded away. I took a deep breath of sea air and just when I thought I was doing better, I began to think of Elliott's death again. I was hoping I could grind it down into nothing like I did with Julian's mom, but I was still too upset, and even though I took an extra walk up and down the dunes I couldn't get my anger and sadness to go away.

When I came through the front door I knew Mom had been waiting for me.

"Where've you been?" she asked, looking me right in the eyes before I could look away.

"Just walking on the beach," I said, "thinking."

"You were off brooding," she guessed. "Tell me the truth."

"Maybe a little," I replied.

"Your dad *broods*," Mom said. "You are too young to brood. When something bad happens I want you to have a healthy reaction to it. A strong young man's reaction. I don't want you stewing and getting yourself worked up into a black mood."

"I'm not in a black mood," I said. "I was just trying to feel nothing."

"Feeling *nothing* is not going to solve anything. Now, let's talk," she said, and crossed her hands on her lap. "Tell me how you *feel* about what happened to Elliott." I could tell that she wasn't just going to let me go read *Charlotte's Web* again and think about the life cycle of spiders, and death and rebirth and the natural order of things.

"I'd rather just go sit and think about my problems," I replied. "I'm a man."

"I knew it!" she cried out. "Your dad has already taught you how to brood! You need to talk about this stuff. Both of you need to learn how to talk about stuff that bothers you. Keeping it inside is only going to eat you alive."

"I'll figure it out," I said.

"Not if you listen to him," she said, warning me. "You both need something healthy to do with your time."

"Like what?" I asked.

"I'm not sure yet," she said, standing up and jamming her hands down onto her hips. "But I'll think about it."

Two weeks later Dad and Pete and I got dressed in our new Junior Naval Cadet outfits. Dad had the rank of chief petty officer and we were dressed as new recruits. I guessed Mom was going to set Pete in the right direction while he was still young enough to not fall into the bad habit of brooding. She knew Dad was a lost cause and probably had her fingers crossed that I might come around and see things her way.

Mom lined us up in a row and took our pictures. "My three handsome *men*," she said, as if she were stamping the word *men* on our foreheads. Then we got in Dad's car and quietly drove to Roanoke Island to a sleepover camp for the weekend. If we had any thoughts about what we were doing, we kept them to ourselves. The weekend orientation was supposed to be just for kids from five through eight years old, but Dad brought me along to help, and as Mom said, "Don't worry, you'll fit right in. You're young for your age anyway."

Even before we arrived at the camp I knew it wasn't going to work out very well. First, I was exhausted. I hadn't been sleeping well because I was still so upset about Elliott's dying. I'd lie in bed all night, tossing and turning. At school I kept falling asleep with my head on my desk. When Miss Noelle asked what was wrong I told her I had too much on my mind. She suggested I drink a glass of warm milk before lights out. I looked at her sadly. She didn't understand the private torments of a man. At home I was snappish with Pete and grumpy around Mom. Betsy and I were bickering with each other all day. So I figured that putting on a Naval Cadet uniform and hanging around with a bunch of happy little kids was just going to make me feel worse, and I was right.

On the first night at camp, after a long day of learning how to tie knots, read naval signal flags, and practice Morse code in a dark room with flashlights, we had a cookout. I sat by the bonfire and stuck marshmallows on a stick, set them on fire, then flicked them at the boys. It was like the Roman warship battle scene in *Ben-Hur* when they use catapults to hurl flaming balls of tar at each other's ships. I said to myself, "This is really dangerous," but then another part of me said, "Yeah, but it has something to do with being in the Navy." One flaming sticky ball landed on a kid's hat and set it on fire. Another kid poured a canteen of water on it while I laughed my head off. This should have been a warning that I was getting out of hand, but I was too far gone. All that brooding had made me weak.

The next day I was worse. I hadn't slept a wink and was glaring at anyone who laughed. Dad thought it would be a good idea for me to keep busy, so he gave

me a job. He lined up all the young boys and had me in-
spect their heads for lice. If I found any I was supposed
to call him. He also gave me a set of electric hair clippers and asked me to trim the cadets around their ears
and cut off any hair that touched their collars. But once
he drifted off, I told the boys that if I found lice I would
have to shave their heads.

The first kid who stepped up had a bowl-shaped hair-
cut. I looked down at his blond hair. "Lice!" I declared.
He looked up at me, horrified. "There is only one thing
to do to stop this epidemic," I declared. I took the clippers and in about a minute had buzzed all his hair off.

"That's better," I concluded. "Now beat it!"

He ran his hand over his bald head. "You cut my hair
off," he said angrily.

"What are you going to do about it?" I asked.

He raised his fist and looked like he was going to
jump at me.

"I'll clip your lips off," I said, and waved the clippers
around his face.

The kid backed away. "Don't," he said, suddenly
frightened. He held his hands in front of his mouth.

Somehow, this only made me angrier. "Move it," I
shouted, "or I'll clip your ears off, too." He turned and
ran.

"You better run," I hollered. When I turned around,

all the other kids were fleeing in the opposite direction. Only Pete was left.

"That wasn't very nice," he said.

I raised my fist at him. "You want your other tooth knocked out?" I asked. "Just keep mouthing off to me and you'll be the youngest kid on the planet to wear dentures."

"Bully," he said right back. "You've become a bully but you don't scare me." I stood there with the clippers in my hand as he walked away. I had never been called a bully before, not even by Pete, and I didn't like it. He was right. I *had* been a bully and now I was ashamed of myself, which just seemed to pile on to all the things I was brooding about and not grinding down into *noth-ingness*. I dropped the clippers in the dirt and shuffled over to the chicken-wire fence that surrounded the compound. I looked across at the ocean. The waves churned up the shore, grinding the small grains of sand into even smaller grains. I wondered if they ever got ground down into nothingness, or just got smaller and smaller but never really went away. I attempted to climb the fence, but I couldn't get a toehold in the tight pattern. When I tried to pull myself up, the wire cut into my fingers. I slumped back down. I felt lousy and I didn't know what to do about it.

That night I was tossing and turning in bed as usual.

I couldn't take it anymore. I remembered Dad's advice about taking a walk on the beach. It had helped before when I was angry with Julian's mom. Maybe it would help again.

But there was no way out of the camp. The compound fence was sealed with a locked gate. Little cadets with flashlights and whistles had guard duty, so it was difficult to sneak out. But I thought I had a way. The Dumpsters behind the kitchen were next to the fence. I figured I could climb up one and jump over.

I put on some jeans and a dark T-shirt and sneakers. I tiptoed out of the cabin and away from the security lights. I stood in the shadow of a tree. I looked left and right. The little cadets marched back and forth, patrolling the camp perimeter. I dashed over to another tree. Then another. I could see the mess hall across the square of grass we used for roll call. I checked for guards, then made a dash for a dark corner. But one of the cadets spotted me.

"Halt!" he shouted. "Who goes there?"

I ran around to the back of the building as he blew his emergency whistle. I could hear other whistles. Adult voices shouted out orders. I scampered up on top of the slippery Dumpster. I was a few steps from getting away, but suddenly froze. Directly between me and the fence was a giant raccoon. It had found some uneaten food and was now guarding it with its life. "Shoo!" I hissed. "Beat it!" I waved my arms back and forth. I stomped down on the top of the Dumpster. The raccoon stared at me and rose on its hind legs. It growled. In the light I could see its mouth full of sharp white teeth. In the background I could hear the cadets gathering with the officers.

"He went thataway," a kid hollered. "Behind the kitchen."

The raccoon dropped down and began to inch forward. Behind me, the footsteps were getting closer. There was nothing left to do. I jumped into the Dumpster and quickly tried to cover myself with bags of garbage.

In a moment I was surrounded. Then I got a lucky break. "It's only a raccoon," Dad said. "See—on top of the Dumpster."

"It was a big kid," some cadet said. "I'm sure of it."

But there was also another raccoon. Suddenly I felt something move against my leg and I yelped.

"That's no raccoon," Dad said. "Whoever you are, come on out," he ordered.

I pushed a bag of garbage out of my way. About a dozen flashlights shone on my face. "Look," shouted a kid. "It's the bully."

I scrambled up on top of the bags of garbage and when Dad saw me he hung his head for a moment. Not only was I a bully—something we both hated—but I had also embarrassed him. I was going to have a lot more to brood about.

"Okay," Dad snapped, handing out orders. "The party's over. Everyone back to your posts, or bunks."

"What are you going to do with him?" some kid asked.

Dad didn't answer. "I'll take care of this," he said to the other officers.

After everyone drifted away he turned off his flashlight. "What stupid nonsense were you up to?" he asked.

"I was going to the beach to practice being a man," I said.

"You need some practice," Dad said. "A real man wouldn't end up cornered by a raccoon."

"He was going to bite me," I said.

"I'm ready to do worse to you," he replied. "Now why were you going AWOL?"

"You know," I said. "What you taught me. Brooding with a reason. I was thinking about Elliott and stuff and I was going to walk around the beach and grind it all down to nothingness."

I could tell he didn't want to agree with me, especially after I had embarrassed him in front of everyone. But I also knew he was pleased that I had listened to him.

"I thought we talked through all that Elliott stuff," he said. "I thought you had already ground it down to nothing."

"I guess I still had a little left over," I said. "And now I think I'm becoming a bully."

"Yeah. Pete told me you gave that kid a baldy. Well, maybe we need to add that to our list to talk about," he said.

"But you said that's what Mom does," I said. "Talk, talk, talk."

"Here's a little secret between us," he said. "I don't always like to admit it but your mom is right at least half the time, so let's take a page out of her book and talk about the stuff that's bothering you."

"When?"

"Tomorrow," he said. "Right after I give *you* a baldy, you can start by apologizing to the kids. Then once you mop that up we'll work on Elliott, and it's my guess your bully problem will disappear on its own."

"Thanks for talking about this," I said, "but do I have to get a baldy?"

He rubbed his hand across his chin while he reconsidered. "Your mom would court-martial me if you came home looking like a cue ball."

I smiled up at him. I knew I was off the hook.

"Now, go take a shower!" he barked. "You smell! Then go straight to sleep! No brooding! And that's an order!"

"Yes, sir!" I snapped back. I felt better already.

The Wrong Brothers

Pete and I were trying to be the Wright brothers. He was Orvill and I was Wilbur. I insisted on being Wilbur because of Wilbur the pig from _Charlotte's Web_. We were on the beach with a replica of their bi-wing airplane. They were exactly alike except ours had a rubber band for a motor. I spun the propeller with my finger until the rubber band was as tight as it would go, then I launched it overhead. It took off and really went flying and Pete and I ran after it. Our model flew longer than theirs. In fact,

it flew too long and the wind
took it way out to sea. Then
it crashed.

"Go get it," Pete said.

"No way," I said, "It's ruined."

For a minute we just watched
the seagulls flying and I figured
the Wright brothers did the same.
They must have been jealous. Then
we went ~~~

sh ## Second Infancy It
Free ~~~ car~ ~ you
shop lift.

"What are they giving away
for free?" Pete asked. His reading
still wasn't so good.

"Police car rides for stealing,"
I replied. Then we went into
the store. I started looking at
the kites because they had

some that looked like planes.
Pete was looking at everything —
keychains, postcards, shells, T-
shirts. I knew he didn't have
and money because he only had
on his bathing suit. And then
I saw him steal something. I couldn't
tell what it was, but it was small
enough to hide it under his arm-
pit and keep it there with
his arm pressed to his side.
        "Pete!" I whispered. He turned
and looked at me. I didn't
know if I should say something
about what he was doing. I
walked over toward him. "Give
me that," I said and held out
my hand. He raised his arm and
a big shark tooth fell to the
floor. "I just want the free ride," he

I was staring at her again. Miss Noelle. I had my elbows propped up on my desk and my head in my hands and I was quietly murmuring everything she said with my lips just parted like a ventriloquist. When she would stop and cock her head to one side, trying to catch who was making the tiny buzzing sounds, I would stop. She'd start. I'd start. She'd talk quickly. I'd buzz quickly. She'd suddenly go slow. I'd go slow. It was as if I were in a very fast car, hugging the road, speeding along the straightaways, downshifting on the curves, leaning left and right, sticking with the road like glue as my senses entirely focused on imitating every contour of her ribbon of words. It was exhilarating. I imagined driving my silver-and-black convertible Porsche with Miss Noelle in the front seat. The wind whipped through our hair. The golden sun reflected off her tinted glasses. She snapped open her purse and pulled out a lipstick. I kept the car steady as she slid the lipstick back and forth across her red lips. She had total confidence in my driving ability. Somehow, I had been a Le Mans race-car driver before I met her. I was skilled, and as I drove, with one black driving glove on the wheel and the other on the gearshift knob, I seamlessly slipped through the gears and steered through the pull of the hairpin turns. We were in the Swiss Alps, on a skiing trip. We were driving up from the south of France where we had just been to a film festival. My new movie was being praised. I was the star. Everyone in the entire *world* wanted to be with me. But I only wanted to be with Miss Noelle.

"Jack," Miss Noelle said sharply, appearing suddenly in front of my desk. "Have you listened to a word I said about our Outer Banks science projects?"

"No, Miss Noelle," I said in a practiced voice. "I was already thinking way ahead to our next assignment."

She leaned down close to my ear. "I don't believe you. See me after class," she said.

Automatically my lips buzzed, *"See me after class."*

"What?" she asked sharply.

"I look forward to seeing you after class," I replied, smiling innocently.

She took a long deep breath then turned back to the class and continued to describe what nature the Wright brothers had first found when they arrived on Cape Hatteras in 1900. I tried to listen. I looked directly up at her face. I watched her lips open and close. I heard the words float out of her mouth and then slowly I drifted back to thinking about our great life together driving up and down the mountain peaks of the Alps. I just couldn't help it.

At the end of the day I eagerly waited for everyone to leave the room. I pulled a chair up to the other side of her desk and stared at her. "I'm *seeing* you after class," I said sweetly, "just as you asked. See, I was listening."

She frowned. "You listen selectively," she replied.

"I'm picky," I explained.

"You're slipping," she said, leaning forward with her elbows on her desk. "Instead of becoming more mature, you are going backward. You're acting like a baby."

"No, I'm not," I said. "A baby would cry. I'm smiling."

"Believe me, you are acting like a baby," she repeated. "You are spending too much time thinking about me, and not enough time thinking about what I'm trying to teach you."

"No," I said.

"What wildlife did the Wright brothers find on the Outer Banks?" she asked quickly. "What?"

"Mosquitoes?" I guessed. "Sand fleas?"

She shook her head in disgust. "You are becoming a love *pest*!" she hissed. "So I set up an appointment for you with the school psychologist."

That chilled me. I had never talked to a psychologist

before. Dad always called them head shrinkers. He claimed that anyone who went to one was crazy before they saw one and had to be locked up in a padded cell after they saw one. "Do I have to?" I asked.

"Either that," she said, "or I'll have Mrs. Nivlash transfer you to another class."

That got me. "Okay," I said, squirming in my chair. "Okay, I'll see the shrink."

"Psychologist," she said, correcting me.

"Psychologist," I buzzed.

Mrs. Rutland, the psychologist, shared a small office with the county health officer. They took turns doing pretty much the same thing. The health officer picked through the hair on my head, searching for lice and other vermin. Mrs. Rutland was going to stare into my head and pick through my brain looking for loose screws, stripped gears, and other signs of madness.

When I sat down I smiled at her and crossed my hands on my lap. She reminded me of my mother. She was neatly dressed, but not overdressed, her hair was done at home and not in a beauty parlor, and her hands were red, I imagined, from doing dishes. The first thing she said was, "If you lie to me, I cannot help you."

"I won't lie," I replied, as if she already had me wired up to a lie detector.

Then she asked me a few questions about myself and

my family before she cleared her throat and got to the point. "Miss Noelle says you seem to have an *infatuation* with her."

"Yes," I said, spitting out the answer as if my life depended on it.

"Can you stop having this infatuation?"

"No," I snapped.

"Have you been fantasizing about her?"

"Yes," I said.

"Do you know this is unhealthy?"

"Yes," I replied.

"Check," she confirmed, making a large check mark in the air with her finger. "Do you mistake Miss Noelle for your mother?"

"No!" I said.

"Do you think she will give you better grades if you are nice to her?"

"I never thought of that," I replied.

"Have you ever given her a gift?"

"No," I said, thinking that flowers taken from a grave site did not count as a gift.

"You can relax," she ordered. "There's nothing wrong with you."

"Are you sure?" I thought if I was slightly off my rocker it would make me seem more sympathetic to Miss Noelle, as if she had to be more sensitive to my special needs.

"Believe me," Mrs. Rutland said, jotting a few notes on a school health form. "Boys like you need a hobby. Something to keep your mind trained on other things besides Miss Noelle. I think a pet would help you."

"I'd like a pet," I said. "But my parents won't go for it. They said three kids and tadpoles is enough pets already."

"You'll just have to try harder to convince them," she persisted. "Tell them you need one in order to focus your *boy* energy in the proper direction." She ripped the health form off the pad and handed it to me. "This is your pet prescription," she explained. "Once you get a pet, have your parents sign the bottom of this form and return it to me." She stood up.

"I still don't think they'll go for it," I pleaded.

"You either get a pet," she said directly, "or I'll send an official note home to your parents telling them I think you are immature for your age and need to be held back a year. And believe me, if you repeat fourth grade you will *not* have Miss Noelle."

I tried to say something else, but she cupped her hands around her mouth and yelled out, "Next!" There was a line of other kids waiting and I guessed my five minutes of mental health were up, which was fine with me.

That night at the dining room table I decided not to tell everyone about my infatuation problem and pet prescription. Instead I said, "I think if I had a pet it would help me become more mature."

"Getting a brain transplant might help," Betsy suggested.

"You could get a new brain but I'm still not having a pet in this house," Mom said. "They are dirty—filthy, really—and carry diseases. Plus we don't have room for one."

"But it will help me be more *mature*," I said, sitting up properly in my seat and crossing my hands on my lap. But she wasn't listening to me.

"And another thing," she said. "No matter what your father intends, he never helps out with a pet. It always ends up being my responsibility."

She was right. When I was about five Dad came home with some kind of used hunting dog that had accidentally been shot and was now afraid of gunfire. He said it would make a great kid pet. It did. I pulled on its ears as if they were taffy. I rode it around the house. I made it eat bugs, and the dog never snapped at me. But Dad seldom took care of it. He didn't walk it, exercise it, pick up after it, feed it, or take it to the vet for shots, and finally after Mom had given him a few warnings she gave it to a family down the street.

I thought maybe Dad was still resentful of that and so I looked to him for help. "How 'bout it, Dad, can I get a pet?"

"I agree with your mother," he said without a second thought. "We don't need a pet. It's one or the other—kids or pets—and we have decided to keep you three rather than turn you in for a litter of pups." He smiled as Mom nodded approvingly.

"I can't believe you agree with Mom," I said. "You two never agree on anything."

"Well, we agree hand in glove on this issue," he said. "No pets."

"So that means you will have to go," Betsy said, pointing at me. "I'll call the vet and see if she can find you a nice new home."

"I wish she could find me a new home," I said, so hurt that I meant it. If someone had asked if I wanted to roll the dice and maybe end up living with another family, I would have taken the chance. What did I have to lose? A house trailer that didn't fit us. A little swamp that smelled like a backed-up toilet. A tough older sister who patrolled the house like a hungry shark. A little brother who thought he was a genius but was really a nuisance. And parents who spent more time telling me what I couldn't do than what I could do. I was ready to let the vet give me my shots and put my photo on her GOOD HOMES NEEDED bulletin board.

But before I could get her a picture to put up, she got in touch with me first. The next day the phone rang and I picked it up.

"Henry residence," I sang into the mouthpiece.

"Remember your duck, Quack?" she asked right away.

How could I forget? She had made me clean smelly cages for two weeks as payment for flipping his feet around. "Yes," I replied. "How's he doing?"

"His feet are fine, but he seems a bit depressed. I think he needs some help building up his self-esteem."

"What do you mean, *building up his self-esteem*?" I asked.

"I mean, he is feeling insecure from having such a rough start in life and I think you should help build up his confidence."

"How?" I asked. I just couldn't imagine what I'd have to do to make a duck feel more self-confident.

"There's a Pet Parade coming up," she said. "You march Quack in the parade and if he is the best-looking pet, he wins a blue ribbon. And that would make him feel better, I'm sure."

"Would a duck even know he had won something?" I asked. "I mean, how does a duck know about *self-esteem*?"

"Animals are very mysterious," she said carefully. "Researchers are not yet sure what they feel and don't feel. But one thing they have in common with humans is that they respond to love and attention, and that leads to better self-esteem."

"Well," I said, "are his feet strong enough to make it through a whole parade?"

"They are facing front and center," she said, like she was captain of the duck brigade. "And they are fully healed and ready to waddle."

"Are you sure this will work?" I asked.

"It can't hurt," she reasoned.

"I have one little problem," I said sheepishly. "My parents won't let me have a pet."

"He's not a house pet," she said. "You can keep him outside in a plastic kiddie pool."

"We have a little swamp," I suggested. "Will that work?"

"Perfect!" she said. "You can think of him as an animal that you are reintroducing into the wild."

That sounded like a good science project for Miss Noelle. "Okay, I'll take him to the parade."

"He'll need a little work," she said. "You'll have to groom him."

"Sure," I replied, not having any idea what went into grooming a duck for a contest. But I figured it couldn't be much, and then he'd be gone.

I was wrong. When I went over to her office to get Quack, he looked like he had been living in an oil slick. He was filthy. His lower beak was still scratched up from hitting the pavement, and there were two thick red scars where his little legs had been broken and twisted back into place.

"He looks awful now," she said, picking at his stubby gray feathers, "but you have a few weeks to get him ready."

"Weeks?" I said. "I thought I'd just take him to the parade, build up his self-esteem, and then he'd fly off with the other ducks. My parents won't let me have him for weeks."

"You'll have to talk them into it," she said. "Because it will take weeks to artificially stimulate his winter plumage to grow so he'll look plump and clean and healthy."

"How do I do that?" I asked, knowing I wasn't going to like the answer.

"Every day you put him in the freezer for five minutes. That's all it takes. Just five minutes of winter weather, and you'll see, after a few days new feathers will start growing."

I couldn't believe my ears. "My mother will kill me if I put a duck in her freezer. Please don't make me do that," I pleaded.

"Where there's a will, there's a way," she said breezily, then got back to grooming the duck. "Just before the contest you'll have to polish up his beak and feet."

"With what?" I asked.

"Car polish," she said. "It's the best."

"And what about the scars and scratches?"

"Wax crayons should help," she suggested. "Don't you know anything about grooming animals for contests?"

I didn't. It was all I could do to take a shower, brush my teeth, and comb my hair each day. I hadn't polished my shoes all year, and now I was going to have to buff a duck's feet until looking at them made you squint. And worse, I was going to have to sneak him into Mom's freezer every day. If she caught me, she'd kill me. And if Betsy caught me, she'd never believe I was trying to get his winter feathers to grow. She would accuse me of torturing animals by freezing them to death. Even Dad would think it was weird. And the only reason I wasn't afraid of Pete is because if he caught me I'd threaten to put *him* in the freezer, and that would keep him quiet.

"One more thing," I said to the vet. "Could you sign this paper?" It was my pet prescription. "The school shrink wants me to have a pet," I said.

"I can see why," she remarked. "Taking care of a pet might be good for *your* self-esteem."

Little did she know. Walking a duck on a leash in a public parade is going to crush my self-esteem, I thought, as she signed with a flourish. Next year the duck will have to walk me.

———

On the way home I renamed him King Quack because I thought it would be good for his self-esteem to come from royalty. When I got him home I tied one of his legs to a small tree outside. I decided to take the direct approach with Mom and Dad instead of trying to be sneaky. As soon as I entered the house I looked at them and said, "I have something *unbelievable* to tell you."

"Try me," Mom replied.

I told them about King Quack and his self-esteem problem and how I was going to help him out with the parade. "We'll only have him for three weeks," I promised. "Only three and then he goes."

"We used to eat ducks," Dad said. "Pluck 'em and grill 'em."

"He's not the eating kind," I said. I knew Dad was thinking that if we ate him it would save money. One less chicken to buy.

"You can't bring him in the house," Mom said sternly.

"I promise he'll never step foot inside," I said, knowing that I was lying a little bit because I had to put him in the freezer and, technically, the freezer was inside. But I would carry him.

"Well," she considered, "taking care of an animal is a *maturing* experience."

"And it will be good for my self-esteem if I do a good job," I said.

Mom leaned forward and gave me a kiss. "I think

you're right," she said quietly. "But just for three weeks."

"Thanks," I said.

After dinner Dad got me some chicken wire and I made a cage for King Quack out on the edge of the swamp so he wouldn't walk or swim off, and so no other animals would hurt him.

That night, once I was sure everyone had gone to sleep, I sneaked down the hall and out the side door. I walked over to King Quack. He was sleeping. I took the big rubber band out of my pajama pocket and quickly reached down and snapped it across his beak. "No quacking allowed," I whispered, "or I'll be living out here with you, and Dad will be thinking of how to pluck and grill me."

I quickly carried him inside and opened the freezer door. "Don't worry," I said. "I'll be right here."

I set him in and closed the door and started counting the seconds. "One thousand one, one thousand two, one thousand three . . ."

Suddenly Betsy walked down the hall and saw me. "What are you doing?" she asked, heading for the bathroom.

"Just getting a drink of water," I rasped with a fake parched voice. When she left I had no idea how much time had passed. I skipped a minute and started counting down two hundred and forty seconds. When I heard the toilet flush I squatted in the shadows. Betsy padded down the hall and went back to her room. I forgot how much time passed again so I skipped another minute. When I had counted down one hundred and eighty seconds I opened the freezer door. King Quack was in the same spot where I had left him. "Sorry," I whispered. I pulled him out and held him in my arms. He was really cold, but I wanted him to know that I cared about him. I tucked him under my pajama top so that we would be cold together.

I kept this up for a whole week without getting caught. But one day Mom was waiting for me when I came home from school.

"I found *this* in the freezer," she said, holding up a duck feather.

"Oh, I can explain," I said, trying to think fast. "It must have been stuck on my shirtsleeve and fallen off when I reached in for a Popsicle."

"What about the webbed footprints?" she asked, and opened the freezer door. "Well?" There were footprints all over the TV dinners.

I broke down and told her everything. "I know it sounds odd," I said, "but it's supposed to work. In fact I think it *is* working. I saw some new white feathers poking through the dirty ones."

"It sounds sick," she said.

"I'm just following directions from the vet," I said. "She wouldn't want me to do anything dangerous."

Mom gave me a perplexed look. "Well," she said, throwing her hands up into the air, "at least put some socks on him when you put him in the freezer." Then she walked down the hall mumbling to herself. "I must be losing my mind," she said over and over.

The next two weeks were strange. On the one hand, getting the duck ready for the parade was about the weirdest thing I ever did. But on the other hand, as a result of taking care of him, feeding him, petting him, cleaning him, giving him his top-secret five minutes of winter weather in the freezer with doll socks on in the middle of the night, I fell absolutely in love with him. While I talked to him in baby-duck talk and cared for him, my mind began to drift and I found myself thinking about my family and how much I loved them, too. Especially Pete. I was the older brother and here I was spending more time taking care of a duck than I was my own brother. I petted the duck. I never petted Pete. I hugged the duck. I never hugged Pete. I gave the duck good advice—*don't blow your nose under your wing*—*stay away from dogs that are foaming at the mouth*—*stand with your head up and shoulders back*—*keep your beak closed unless you are speaking*—*always walk in a straight line with purpose*—*sleep only while floating in the middle of a pond.* The only advice I gave Pete was to stay on his side of the room, not to speak to me unless I spoke to him first, and not to run through the house with his toothbrush in his mouth because if he fell down he could drive it through the back of his head.

And to my surprise I began to think of Betsy, too. I hadn't been very nice to her either. When she left the house I'd sneak into her room and move all her things around. I put dead bugs in the toes of her shoes. I glued pages of her diary together. I erased the phone numbers in her address book and made up phony ones. When her friends stopped by to visit, I began to fake cry and told them we were just on our way to the hospital to claim her body which had been identified only from dental records. It occurred to me that I no longer knew how all our meanness had started. Was I mean to her first, and was she mean as a result? Or was she mean first, and was I mean in retaliation? I didn't know, but it was worth thinking about.

I knew Dad thought I was a bit of a loser. But if I listened to him and did what he wanted me to do once in a while, I thought he would lighten up on me. When I borrowed tools from him I never put them away properly and left them all over the house and yard. And when I washed the car I always managed to leave his window cracked open and soak his seat so the next time he sat down the bottom of his pants got all wet. He didn't like that—especially when the guys at work teased him about peeing in his pants. And every time he asked me to get something for him I always said, "In a minute." After a few times of saying that in a row, he would get steamed at me for not being respectful. He was right. I just wasn't that helpful. He was trying to make ends meet and provide a good home and I was just letting everything unravel.

And with Mom I figured if I helped around the house more without always having to be told what to do ten times in a row, and stopped my whining and complaining while I did anything useful, then I bet she would be in a better mood and have more fun with me instead of looking at everything I needed as a big chore for her. She was counting the days until Dad finished his duty and we could move off this "sand dune," and I was just making each day longer for her instead of shorter.

I looked at my little duck and thought he was very good medicine. The psychologist was a lot smarter than I thought. Taking care of a pet was making me feel very *mature*.

The morning of the parade I got up early, before anyone else. I put on my clean jeans and a white T-shirt and sneakers. I went outside and got King Quack out of his cage. First, I fed him a couple slices of stale bread. As he ate I examined his feathers. They were fuller and clean. When he finished eating I sat him on my lap. I polished his beak and feet with car wax that I took from Dad's trunk. I had to use only a little bit and he shone right up with the buffing cloth. The scratches on his beak seemed okay to me so I left them alone, and his red scars were fine. I thought they were decorative, kind of like red lightning-bolt tattoos. I figured if he looked clean and healthy and happy, then that was the best we could do. Even if he didn't win a blue ribbon, he knew I loved him. I put his glitter collar on that I had bought at the pet store and snapped on his matching leash. He looked great to me.

The parade was down at the fishing pier. By the time we arrived about fifty kids with their pets were gathered in the middle of the street. There were mostly dogs, but I also saw two goats, a pig, a lot of cats, some parrots, snakes, a jumping frog, a pony, a ferret, and a skunk that had been descented. There were no other ducks. We all had to sign in and declare what category we were competing in. There was no listing for ducks, so I put my name down under "Waterfowl." Finally, a man dressed up as Dr. Dolittle announced the beginning of the Pet Parade! He began to march down the street with a cockatoo perched on his outstretched finger. The streets were lined with cheering people. Some of them I knew from school. First, the dogs were called to march. They lined up. Some were dressed with bandannas

around their necks and little party hats. One pulled a
wagon with a toddler in the back. Then the cats were
called. They went every which way. The goats were
oblivious of everything except trash on the streets,
which they tried to eat. The pig drew the most attention. His owner, a young girl, had dressed him up in a
little sailor outfit, but he was still *Wilbur* to me.

Finally, it was our turn. I squatted down and gave
King Quack a pat on his head. "This is your big moment," I whispered. "Let's show 'em what you're made
of." And we walked with our heads held high down the
center of the street. King Quack looked to the left and
right and quacked to his audience as he waddled hap-
pily down the street. We were cheered every step of the
way. My chest was puffed out with pride and when we
passed by Mom and Dad and Pete and Betsy and they
hollered out "Hail, King Quack!" I thought my cheeks
would burst. King Quack waddled and stretched his
wings, and his beautiful new white feathers reflected the
sun. People stepped out of the crowd and took photo-
graphs of us and I thought it was the greatest moment
of my life.

After we got our blue ribbon, the vet came up to me.
"You did it," she said. "Just look at him. He looks so
happy."

"Yes," I said, "and I think we are going to keep him."

"You can't," she said. "He has to go find some other

ducks and live with them. He's grown up now and it's time for him to move on."

"How will he find them?" I asked.

"Just leave him outside, uncaged," she said. "He's feeling good now and before long he'll join up with other ducks around town."

"Are you sure?" I asked. "I know he had a rough beginning to his life, and I just want to keep helping him."

"You have to let him go," she said. "You gave him all the help he needs to feel good about himself. Now he just has to do what ducks do."

"Without me?"

"Without you," she said.

We took him home and pampered him through the weekend but on Monday morning I took the chicken-wire cage down and left him alone. "Take your time and stick around here if you want," I said. "But I'll understand if you need to get on with your duck life." I knelt down and placed his blue ribbon on the ground by the side of the water.

"Quack," he said.

"Quack," I said back, and went on to school.

Miss Noelle had moved my desk to the back of the class and was kind enough to face it toward the window so I didn't have to look at a wall all day. For the three weeks while I took care of King Quack I didn't get lovesick about her at all. I listened to what she was teaching us, and I did my work, but mostly I thought about King Quack.

It happened right after lunch. I had just sat down at my desk for ten minutes of quiet reading when I looked up from my book and out the window. I saw a white duck flying away in the distance and wondered if it was King Quack. Then the sun struck at just the right angle and I saw a bright reflection of light flash off its beak and feet. That must be him, I said to myself, he's the most well-polished duck in town. I watched as he turned and then flapped his wings and became smaller and smaller, until I couldn't see him anymore. And then that sad feeling came over me. He was gone. But at least he was doing what ducks do—going to find other ducks.

Suddenly I looked up into the sky. "Look out for hunters," I said. "I forgot to tell you about them."

When reading time was over I knew my big test was coming. King Quack was gone. And with his departure I was free to think my romantic thoughts about Miss Noelle again. I put one of King Quack's feathers between the pages of my book to mark my place, then turned to listen to what she had to say about our science projects. As I listened, I rubbed the feather between my fingers. It was like rubbing a lucky charm. But it was a funny charm because it worked in reverse. Wishes came true before I even wished for them. I got over Miss Noelle and I never thought I wanted to. But now my crush had disappeared and my time was spent thinking about real things rather than some silly fantasy of me and her driving through the Alps. And I began to look forward to going home so I could be nicer to everyone, because it was suddenly obvious that the nicer I was to them, the nicer they were in return. And finally I realized that *I* was the one who could have used a little boost to my self-esteem, and as a result I was more mature. King Quack had helped me more than I had helped him.

I looked out the window again. King Quack was long gone. But what he left behind was still in me. I loved that duck.

My Life as I Wish
it Would Be...

When I walk down the
street people would say,
   "There goes that handsome
Jack."
   "That Jack is so smart."
   "He is the nicest boy in
the world."
   "Jack is the king of the
surfing world."
   "Jack Henry is the all time
winner of everything."
   "He can read minds. Watch
what you think!"
   "Did you know that Jack
Henry has walked more old
people across the road than

any other kid."

"That Jack Henry is a famous kid astronaut."

"He's so much more clever than his sister."

"Did you know he climbed Mt. Everest?"

"And he was the youngest captain of a submarine."

"H   ives advice to the p

"His   ith sports trophies."

"Did you hear that he is skipping fifth, sixth, seventh, eighth and ninth grade?"

"He alredy has a driver's license."

"Built his own car!"

"Hollywood is making a

movie of his life."

"He speaks a dozen foreign languages."

"I heard James Bond is jealous of him."

"Have you seen him tame sharks?"

"The National Gallery just purchased one of his paintings."

"Today I heard his hit song on the radio."

"How can he be so fabulous and still be so nice?"

"His head is screwed on correctly."

"always puts one foot in front of the other."

"His moral judgements were noticed by the pope."

"What a saint!"

I was sitting at the dining room table doing a book report on a famous American flier, but I wasn't writing very much. I was thinking that getting a C on the report was good enough. In class, Miss Noelle had made up a list from the Wright brothers to Amelia Earhart to Charles Lindbergh—one flier for each kid. She gave me Will Rogers and said I reminded her of him because he was an "odd duck." I looked at his picture and was disappointed because he was not very handsome. He had a wide, goofy-toothy smile and a piece of hay sticking out the corner of his lips. She didn't tell me he had died in a plane crash either.

Reluctantly I began reading about him and before long I found he was so funny that, to anyone who would listen, I kept quoting things he had said. I wasn't getting much writing done, but reading his quotes was great fun. "Everything is funny as long as it is happening to

somebody else," he had said. That seemed true. At
school I saw a kid puke on another kid and I laughed
about it all day. But it wouldn't have been funny if he
had puked on me. And Will Rogers also had said, "Live
your life so that you wouldn't mind selling your pet par-
rot to the town gossip." That struck me as something to
write down and keep in mind.

Then, like a sudden gale blowing through, Betsy and
I got into an argument over one of his quotes. Will
Rogers had said he'd "rather be the man who bought
the Brooklyn Bridge than the man who sold it." I
agreed with him.

"Only an idiot could agree with that," she argued.
"How can you be so stupid? The guy who buys the
Brooklyn Bridge—which *can't* be bought—gets nothing.
And the guy who sells it gets all the money."

"That's not the point," I said. "It's not about money.
It's about being a good person. He's saying he'd rather
be gullible than be a crook. He'd rather be nice than be
a creep."

"Well," she said, "I'd rather be rich than be an
idiot."

Dad heard everything from where he was sitting in
the living room. "I agree with your sister," he called out.
"Besides, Will Rogers is overrated. He said he never
met a man he didn't like. *Who* could believe that? I meet

some yo-yo every day I could run down in the street and never see again."

Mom was down the hall cleaning the bathroom, but she could hear every word we said. "Well, I agree with young Jack," she called out. "I'd rather be a bit naïve and buy the Brooklyn Bridge and always see the good in people than be a rich crook who spends his miserable life thinking the world is filled with people to take advantage of."

"Look at it this way," Dad reasoned. "Rich people have a choice. They can see the good in people or the bad because they have the *time* to sit around and pick the lint out of their belly buttons. Poor people have to *work* all day long."

It was kind of interesting listening and watching Mom and Dad debate with each other, even though they weren't in the same room. It really didn't seem like an argument. It seemed more like theater. And I knew, sort of, what they were going to say as if I had seen the play before.

"There is nothing wrong with honest hard work," Mom continued, while scrubbing the toilet.

"But after you work for the Navy day in and day out, you begin to wish you had a few extra bucks," Dad said.

"I don't have to work for the whole Navy to dream of a few extra bucks," Mom said.

"Now don't start again about me not making enough money," Dad said, with his voice rising.

Mom must have grimaced. Money was an issue. "I wish you would just listen to yourself," she said.

"I can't listen to myself," Dad snapped back. "I'm always busy listening to you."

"And just what do you mean by that!" Mom said sharply, and stuck her head out of the bathroom to glare down the hallway.

Betsy gave me a weary look that said she was totally tired of me. "See what you started again," she whispered.

"I mean," Dad considered, calming down a bit, "that I'm always listening to your good advice. Why just last week I took a page out of your book."

"How so?" Mom asked suspiciously.

"My commanding officer asked me how I felt about being in the service and I told the *truth*, and nothing but the truth. In so many words I told him this Navy job was for the birds. And guess what? He turned around and took a page out of my book. He told me exactly what I wanted to hear—that *I* was for the birds. Then he offered me an early release and I took it. Signed on the dotted line."

Mom marched down the hall with the toilet brush held tightly in her yellow-gloved hand. She looked shocked. "We'll stay on till the end of the school year, won't we?" she asked.

"Yeah," he replied. "It will take a while for the discharge paperwork to come through and by then school should be over and we can stop living in this sardine can and move on to greener pastures."

"Well, I can't argue with that," she said. "But what kind of discharge are you getting?"

He sort of looked the other way, as if someone were calling him, but I knew he didn't want to look Mom in the eye.

"An O-T-H," he said quickly.

"I've never heard of that before," she said. "What's it mean?"

"Other Than Honorable," he said casually. "It just means that we have agreed to go our separate ways. They neither love me nor hate me. It's neutral."

"Why aren't you getting an honorable discharge?" she asked.

"Let's just say," Dad replied, "that every day I showed up for work I complained, until I finally wore them down and now they've decided to set me free to do what I want to do."

"And now they think you are a lousy worker," she said.

"What's it matter? I'll never see them again."

"Maybe so, but what about your self-pride?"

"I never let pride stand in the way of what I want," he said. "If some people think I'm a jerk, that's fine with me as long as I can get what I want."

"Well, I'd rather be able to hold my head up high in front of any kind of people."

"Hey, I'd just rather head on out," he said. "Out of sight, out of mind. That's my rule."

"And one I should put to use right now," she said, turning and marching back down the hall.

I was just imagining what Act II might be between Mom and Dad, when Betsy slowly stood up and leaned over me.

"Hold still," she cautioned, as she raised her open hand behind her head. "This is going to sting, but don't think about it or you'll twitch."

Then she cut loose. *Slap!* She smacked me across my ear. I thought I'd been hit with a baseball bat. My Will Rogers book flew to the other side of the room and I slipped off the edge of my chair.

"Why'd you do that?" I yelped, and hopped up.

"Mosquito," she said. "They carry yellow fever. I may have saved your life."

"I think you just wanted to hit me because you're in a bad mood," I said.

She scoffed. "Check your ear," she ordered.

I wiped my finger over my stinging ear, then looked at it. There was blood.

"See," she said. "I nailed a big fat one. You should thank me."

"For puncturing my eardrum?" I replied.

"No," she argued. "I killed something that had obviously *punctured* you."

I didn't want to believe her. I wanted to think she was just mean enough to suddenly haul off and swat me around the room like a tetherball. But she was right. We were having a big mosquito problem. They were everywhere. At night they were matted up against the window screens like a fur coat. Mom kept citronella candles lit around the doorways, but that didn't scare them off. When the front door opened, mosquitoes poured in like water. We chased them around the house with rolled-up newspapers, flyswatters, and slippers. Some mosquitoes were so full of blood that when we smashed them against the wall, they splattered like tiny balloons full of paint. Mom patrolled behind us and washed the splat marks off the wall, but I could still see a faint gray-and-red stain left behind.

With everyone in such a bad mood, I went outside to sit. I'd rather fight with mosquitoes, I thought while rubbing my ear, than with my family. I sprayed myself with bug repellent and stood next to the swamp. The mosquitoes buzzed around my face but they didn't like the kerosene smell of the spray. When I looked east it was already dark. When I looked west the sky seemed to have a purplish black eye. It was hard not to think about the differences between Mom and Dad. For Mom, life was about being a good person and living with pride. Dad just wanted to get ahead any way he could. I wished I could be both of them, and get ahead *with* pride. But by the way they talked you had to choose to be one or the other—not both. I knew we would leave Cape Hatteras but I should try harder to "live up to my potential and get better grades" as Miss Noelle had put it. Just because I knew I would never see her again didn't mean I could slack off.

I looked out at the mosquitoes. They were rising up from the swamp like clouds of black smoke. "It's going to be life or death for you guys," I shouted. "You can't choose both!" I stepped forward and sprayed at a cloud of them. A few with drenched wings fell into the water and struggled until a small frog popped up from the swampy ooze and swallowed them. But no matter how many I killed, or were eaten, we couldn't keep up with how rapidly they were hatching. Mom had called the health department and they had promised to come out and spray the swamp, but the epidemic was everywhere and the spray trucks were busy in rich neighborhoods.

It was a relief to me when Julian came out of his

house wearing a khaki explorer's hat with mosquito net-
ting that covered his entire head and was tucked into
the neck of his T-shirt.

"Guess what-what-what!" he hollered.

"You're going on a safari," I replied.

"No," he said, grinning. "We're moving. My-my-my
dad quit the Navy."

"You can't just quit," I said.

"I know," he said. "I mean my dad is going to get out
early and we're going to move to Vicksburg."

"When are you going? Because my dad quit, too."

"Next week. He's sending us away first and he'll join
us later."

"It was nice knowing you," I said sadly.

"I'm not gone-gone-gone yet," he replied. "We still
have a week to do weird stuff."

"What do you want to do?"

"My dad said I can have all his model warships. He
and I put together a whole fleet of them this year but
he's so sick and tired of the Navy, he says he never
wants to see another ship again."

"What do you want to do with them?"

"Let's have a global total war destruction sea battle,"
he gushed. "You get your ships and we'll get some fireworks and blow them to kingdom come."

"Cool," I said.

"You have any money?" he asked.

"A few bucks."

"Bring it tomorrow," he said. "We'll go down to the Big Bang Barn and buy them after class. They sell *lethal* stuff."

"Okay," I said. "Tomorrow we'll have a blowout. The last ship floating rules the world."

"There won't-won't-won't be a winner," he said. "We'll destroy the entire planet. There'll be nothing left of Earth but a cloud of toxic space dust."

"Can we leave Earth and colonize another planet?" I asked.

"Only if you have big-big-big bucks," he said. "My dad said poor people are the first to go in a war."

"Julian!" his mother called out. "Get in here before you get infected with equine encephalitis."

"What's that?" I asked.

"Horse fever," he replied. "Your brain swells up and your head pops."

"Julian!" she called again, and he took off running.

When I went back into my room I looked over at my ship models. I had an aircraft carrier, the *Kitty Hawk*. A submarine, the *Narwhal*. A command ship, the *Coronado*. And a few World War II battleships along with my favorite model—PT-109, President Kennedy's torpedo boat that was rammed and sunk by a Japanese ship in the South Pacific. It had taken me all year to save up for them and build them but now, like Dad, I was ready to blow my Navy away—ready to sink the lot of them and move on to other battles.

The next day after school we went down to the Big Bang Barn.

"Let me do the talking," Julian said, as we opened the door. "I'm a pro."

We walked toward a man sitting at a desk reading the sports page of the newspaper. "What can I do for you, boys," he said, without lowering the paper.

"I was hoping you could sell us some *ordnance*," Julian said, like he was in the Special Forces.

The man lowered the paper and looked us over pretty good, then smiled. "Just how old are you?"

"Sixteen," Julian replied. "I'm a midget."

"That's good enough for me," the man said. "Now let me see the color of your money."

Julian spread out his life savings, about twenty-five dollars. The man scooped up the bills. "Follow me," he said. We passed by the legal stuff—the sparklers and pinwheels and volcanoes and magic snakes, and then went through a door into a back room. He gave us each a small paper bag. "Start filling up," he said. "I'll tell you when you've hit your limit."

We filled up our bags with the really powerful stuff, and after a few minutes the man said, "Okay, that's enough. You don't want to blow up the whole planet."

"Yes, we do," Julian said.

"Well, have a blast," the man said, and chuckled at himself.

We turned and got out of there as fast as we could. "This is going to be awesome," Julian said on the way home. Then just before we reached our trailers he said, "Take my bag and hide it overnight at your house. My mom will explode if she finds it. Then tomorrow after school we'll have the blowout."

"Okay," I said.

At dinner that night, after we all took our seats and Betsy dimmed the lights to keep the mosquitoes at bay, Mom and Dad started in on Act II of their play. We were eating boiled potatoes with lots of salt, butter, and parsley flakes; pork hot dogs; and celery filled with either peanut butter or Cheez Whiz. Mom had said she was just using up the odds and ends in the refrigerator. Then, in order to get some conversation going, she asked Dad how his day went.

"Crummy," he said, crunching down on the celery. "Dang Navy. They called Julian's dad and me into the front office and gave us a list of all the benefits we won't be eligible for if we take the OTH discharge."

"Did you read the list?" she asked.

"Why bother?" he replied. "I told them if they let me just walk out the door and keep going, then they could keep all their benefits."

"You didn't?" Mom said, shocked.

"Did, too," he replied.

"Well, some of those benefits could help your family," she said indignantly. "Did you ever think of that?"

"Let them rot in you-know-where with their bene-fits," he said, and took a deep breath, and hung his head.

"Why don't you just admit it," Mom said. "You do care what the Navy thinks of you."

Dad's head sprang back up. "I'm not going to let the Navy tell me how I should feel about myself."

"I agree with that," Mom said. "But I don't agree that you don't care. When I know you do."

"Look," he said. "The bottom line is I want out. I don't care if they think I'm a failure or not."

"Then leave with your head held high," she said, "and we won't feel you're a failure either. But you be-have like you are running away with your tail between your legs."

Dad scooted his chair back. "I am not running away," he said sternly.

Mom stood her ground. "You are a quitter," she said. "And a quitter is someone who gets up and runs."

Dad angrily tossed his napkin on top of his plate, stood up, and took a few steps for the door before he re-alized he was doing exactly what Mom had said—run-ning away. "This is my life," he growled. "And I'll live it the way I see fit and I don't need you to tell me what to do, or what is right or wrong. You sound just like the Navy—maybe worse!"

Mom stood up, turned on one foot, and stomped down the hall. Then she stopped and glanced back over her shoulder. "If you can't admit the truth of how you feel about this to me, I can only hope you'll admit it to yourself." Then she walked into the bedroom. Betsy and Pete stood up and followed her.

I looked over at Dad. He shrugged and rested his hand on the doorknob. "Don't worry," he said to me. "The worst that can happen to you is that you grow up to become exactly like your old man." Then he opened the door and, as he left, his place was taken by a dark silhouette of mosquitoes.

That night Dad slept in the car. I know because I stayed awake and waited for him to come home. I heard the car pull up into the yard. The engine stopped. The hot metal ticked. But the car door didn't open, nor did the front door to the house. It confused me that Dad claimed he didn't mind that the Navy thought he was doing a lousy job, because I'm sure he *did* mind. He always complained about people who had no pride in their work. And when I brought my report card home he always read it carefully and, if I received less than an A in any subject, he always accused me of not trying hard enough. And he would end up saying something like, "What's wrong with you? Don't you have any *pride* in your work?"

In the early morning I heard him taking a shower. I got up and went down to the kitchen to get the water started for coffee. I knew he'd need a cup. When I saw him next, I thought he had the measles. He was covered with hundreds of red spots.

"Dang mosquitoes," he said, scratching at his bumpy forearms. "They ate me alive last night."

"I read in the paper where a woman's car broke down in the Everglades and the mosquitoes sucked all her blood out."

"I can believe that," he said glumly. "I think I need a transfusion."

"Coffee's almost ready," I said.

"I'll pick some up on the way to the base," he said quietly. "Before you-know-who gets up and wants the rest of my blood."

"See you later?" I asked.

"Yeah," he said. "Don't worry. I always come around to seeing the better side of things. It just takes me a little longer than most." Then he was out the door.

School was pretty much the same except that something in me had changed. Now that I knew we were going to move, I felt my interest in everyone and everything shrinking. Instead of wanting to hang on tighter, I wanted to let go. Even of Miss Noelle. It was easier that way, to act like people no longer mattered much to me. Maybe Dad was feeling a bit the same. He knew he was pushing off and it was simply easier for him to say he didn't like the Navy rather than say he was going to miss it. I could understand that. I was doing the same thing. As he would say, "You're a lot more like your old man than you'll admit." He was right. I always wanted to believe that I was more like Mom, but when I was honest with myself, I knew there was a lot of Dad in me, too.

After school that day, Julian and I met up as planned and walked home together. Then he went into his house and gathered up his models. I got mine, plus the explosives, and we met back out at the swamp. He positioned his ships on one end of the water and I set up mine. We were only about twenty feet apart.

"Okay-okay-okay!" he shouted. "I wrote a pre–nuclear wasteland song that I want to sing before we get started." He struck his air-guitar pose.

"Sing your atomic anthem," I said.

"Oh, say can you see-see-see," he screeched. "By the dawn's early light. The mushroom cloud-cloud-cloud . . . that turns might into right!" Suddenly he tossed his air guitar to one side and picked up a cherry bomb. "Sneak-sneak-sneak attack!" he shouted. He lit the fuse with a Zippo lighter and threw the first salvo my way. It blew up about an inch above the Kitty Hawk's flight deck. One moment it was an aircraft carrier and after an explosion that knocked me back on my butt, the ship was nothing more than slivers of plastic and gray smoke.

"Direct hit-hit-hit!" he shouted, and lit another.

That got me going. I hopped up and lit three Roman candles at once. "Firing nuke-tipped rockets!" I shouted, and let loose with a neon barrage of fireballs. He kept lobbing cherry bombs and I countered with a string of M-80s. For about two minutes it sounded like a world war.

And then it was over. No ships were left. Pieces of gray plastic floated alongside scraps of red-and-yellow fireworks wrappers. From the blasts, stunned mosquitoes covered the surface of the water like surviving sailors. Then, from below, the frogs gathered to slurp them up like the sharks had done to sailors during the sea battles of World War II.

"Who won?" Julian yelled, fanning the smoke from his face.

"Nobody," I said. "The world as we know it is over."

Suddenly his mom came around the corner. "I told you never to play with fireworks," she said, getting ready to give him a crack.

"It's all his fault-fault-fault!" Julian shouted, pointing at me.

"Don't you lie to *me-me-me*," she said, imitating him. "He's bad," she said, "but *you're* worse."

Then before I could run away my mom opened the side door.

"Jack," she hollered, "what's going on out there? I was in the shower and it sounded like a gunfight."

"Nothing," I replied.

"I swear, you get more like your father every day," she said with disgust in her voice. "Now go to your room."

My room was the one place I wanted to be. It was easy to sit by myself and feel all alone in the world. Like Dad sleeping out in the car, it was easier to just not talk about things that bothered me. It was easier to try to forget my past than to sort it out. It made me sad to think that, like Dad, I was already wanting a part of myself to disappear. I reached across my bed to my nightstand where I had saved one model, PT-109. I pulled it close to me, as if I were keeping it in a safe harbor. I didn't want to let it go. It was a little bit of hope that my year had been worth remembering.

Act III started while Mom cooked dinner. She had a look on her face that told me she was going to tell Dad about my playing with fireworks. But when he came home with a big bouquet of flowers and a card that brought tears to her eyes when she read it, I thought she might decide to give me a break and just go with the good feeling of the evening. Then, when she let him kiss her and give her a back-bending hug, I knew I was in the clear.

Not long into dinner Dad looked at all of us. "It's just hard for me to admit failure," he said. "I wanted this Navy stint to work out but it was a mistake. Like I said before, I don't take orders too well anymore."

"You don't have to tell me that," she said. "I can't even get you to listen to good sense."

He gave her a *don't start that again* look.

"What I mean," she said, "is that you don't have to admit to failure. You just have to tell the truth all the time and then failure is never an issue."

"I don't like to lose at anything," he said.

That reminded me of a Will Rogers quote. "Hey," I said, "Will Rogers said to live your life so that whenever you lose, you're ahead."

Dad gave me a puzzled look. "You know," he said, "for a guy who would rather buy the Brooklyn Bridge than sell it, you really have no ground to stand on when it comes to telling other people how to live their lives."

I wasn't sure if he was just teasing me, or if he was miffed. But Mom came to my defense. "He was only trying to be helpful," she said to Dad.

He looked at me. "With help like that, who needs enemies?"

"Did Will Rogers say that?" I asked.

"No, I did," he replied, and tapped himself on the chest.

I changed the subject. "Julian said his dad is sending them all away before school ends."

"That's because Julian's dad would rather be in an empty house trailer eating TV dinners and drinking cheap beer, with his dirty shoes propped up on the coffee table, than be with his family," Dad said.

"Tell the truth," Mom said. "Don't you envy him?"

"Nope," Dad replied. "I don't. I'd rather hang around here and have my blood sucked out by you human mosquitoes than sit around by myself until I go insane."

"I thought *we* drove you insane," I said, taking advantage of his good mood to ask him an honest question.

"You're too late for that. It's pretty clear to me that I went insane years ago. How else can I explain how I married your mother and had you three wild things?"

"Let's go for a walk along the beach tonight," Mom suggested, and pushed back in her chair.

"What about the mosquitoes?" Betsy asked.

"If you walk along the surf," Mom explained, "the breeze keeps them away."

"Can we stop for ice cream?" Pete hollered.

"Sure," Mom said.

They all stood up and headed for the door.

I stayed in my chair. "Why don't you all go, and I'll just put my feet up and enjoy the peace and quiet?" I suggested.

Dad smiled at me. "You are sounding more like me every day," he said, back-stepping toward me. He reached out and curled his hand around my head and pulled me close to his side. "Keep up the good work and someday you might grow up and realize your old man was a genius."

"You bet," I said.

"Now, let's get this party started," he said, snapping his fingers and doing a little shuffle dance. "Last one to the beach will be sacrificed to the mosquitoes!"

We all lurched for the door and ran out and across the sandy yard, across the warm tar road, and up over the dunes until we could spot the bright path of the rising moon shine over the sea like a silver lining rolling toward the shore. I walked into the surf as the light shimmered around me. For once we didn't have to search for a silver lining. It had found us.